Voyage of the Sea Dragon;

Into the Dream World

By Susan Kite

This is a work of fiction. Any similarity to any persons, living or dead, is coincidental and not intended by the author.

Dedicated to: My darling Dan, who has believed in me from the very first story. Also, to David Hedison, who helped me believe even baffling stories can be taken seriously. And to my critique group, and others who have reined in my imperfections. To my phenomenal editor, Patricia Crumpler. And my thanks to Destin Sandlin of *Smarter Every Day,* who filmed his adventures on an LA class submarine and made me smarter as I wrote about *Sea Dragon*.

Voyage of the Sea Dragon;

Into the Dream World

Chapter One

It will be so good to test the life forms on this planet, the alien master thought. He quivered in excitement, his flat, fist-sized gray body attached securely in the middle of its host's back. *There are so many and they are very dexterous and strong. And young. So many young…*

The host studied a large monitor covering the entire forward wall. Its small dark eyes, sunken under protruding brows, smoldered with eager anticipation. The host was a shaggy, green-haired anthropoid from a distant planet. He couldn't remember what it looked like, and only felt eager for the rest replacement hosts would give him. His only memories were working on the ship and with his host. And his name. They called him Denbra. Or he was a denbra, he couldn't remember which.

The denbra and his kreon master watched as the planet's single large moon eclipsed the orb, the planet filled with life and promise. At an order from its master, the anthropoid reached for the controls with gnarled fingers. They had mounted the control panels around a central round core. There were five control stations, where five kreons, each with their hosts, stood.

The planet came into sharper focus. Data scrolled with irritating slowness along one side of the monitor. The kreon viewed large blue patches of water, spots of green and brown landforms, and white ice and snow under swirling, moisture-laden clouds. All good signs, the master thought hungrily. His body shivered again with excitement.

But they are also intelligent. More intelligent than our normal hosts, another master argued, her thoughts relaying to all in the control room. Her host's fingers were stiffly curled. Its motions were deliberate, slow, and sometimes clumsy. The female master pulsated as she lay on her host's back, centered between its shoulder blades. She knew if there had been other hosts, these old ones—the denbra—would have been retired and allowed to live on a suitable planet until their lives ceased.

However, the masters—the kreon—couldn't release them. There were no new hosts. They had searched worlds and found beings. However, those beings didn't have the means to work the controls or the locomotion—legs—to transport the masters from place to place easily. Others were not compatible. But now? This world surely had beings they could use.

I want us to gather information about the dominant life-form. If they are viable to be hosts, they will supply all we need. And with so many, we'll be able to replicate. Rebuild our race. It has been so long. We have been deprived so long! The hairy arms of the denbra reached for more controls, turned one of them too far and caused the picture to retreat.

You clumsy beast! The master beat into the denbra's brain. They had to get new hosts. The kreon studied the read-outs through denbra eyes that sometimes didn't see clearly. *We'll go down into a remote area and plot our strategy to get these new hosts.* He forced his denbra to clench its fingers so tightly it moaned in pain. *Lay in a course to the continent at the south pole of the planet. There are very few of these creatures there, which will make it easier to experiment on them when we're ready.*

Yes, sir, the other kreons answered. The female kreon directed her denbra to boot up the computer. She had to figure out exactly where on the cold continent they were going to begin their invasion.

Chapter Two

Dr. Richard (Rick) Wilson stood on a pier, studying the behemoth resting serenely in the Naval Station harbor in the Puget Sound. Despite it being stripped of outer decorations and insignia, the submarine amazed him in its size, and powerful in the smooth lines of its hull. A whale without eyes, it remained a child of the sea. At a three hundred and sixty foot length and thirty-three foot beam, something this large could carry scientists all over the world. They could study places previously unknown or inaccessible.

Wilson also considered himself a child of the sea. From Hawaii, the ocean had always been his friend. He felt kinship with the waves and the wind. Average height, he had the physical attributes of a swimmer—lithe and lean. He wore his long, medium brown hair pulled back in a ponytail. Streaks of gray hinted at more than a few years out of college. He balanced on the balls of his feet, like a runner waiting for the starting pistol. Something in this harbor waited to happen. Wilson felt a keyed-up energy building inside.

There were other boats in the harbor, some diesel, a few others nuclear. Wilson only had eyes for this boat, an LA class nuclear submarine recently decommissioned. The nuclear fuel canisters had been removed. The missiles were also gone, but everything else remained intact.

"I always hate seeing one of these boats decommissioned and hauled away for scrap," Admiral Drumwright muttered out of one side of his mouth. The other side shredded a half-smoked cigar. He leaned against the rail, his khaki jacket barely covering his slightly oversized stomach.

Wilson's intense blue eyes shone. He envisioned the submarine as a research vessel that could dive on its own and house scientists with different specialties. They could fulfill many missions. His boat would be self-contained, not tethered to a ship on the surface and beholden to the weather and seasons. A boat like this could do much to learn about the mysterious ocean. "I can't do a thing about the former, but I would sure like to do something about the hauling away part."

"What are you babbling about, Rick?" A slight Southern drawl punctuated the admiral's voice that thirty-plus years of service couldn't quite erase.

"I could take her off your hands." The spring in Wilson's chest continued tightening.

Drumwright laughed. "You're joking, right?"

Wilson shook his head. "I have tried for a half-dozen years to finance building a research submarine."

"I know. Not enough money. Something like that from scratch costs a pretty penny."

"But that hulk down there is only worth scrap now. How much is steel, iron, rubber, and plastic going for these days?"

Drumwright gazed at his companion. "Are you serious?"

"Never more serious in my life. I can take that beautiful hulk and make it a research submarine. It will do what no one with their drone submersibles and dinky surface vessels could dream of doing."

Drumwright tossed the cigar into the bay. "You and what navy?" He sighed. "There is no precedence."

"Jacques Cousteau bought a decommissioned World War II minesweeper and converted it into Calypso."

"Helluva big difference."

Wilson could tell by the tone of the admiral's voice the three-star had not dismissed his dreams. "I know, Admiral, but I need to at least try. The government spends billions on new subs. I only want a chance to build something to study what we've been so blithely taking advantage of and polluting."

"I know what you're saying, Rick, but let me play devil's advocate for a moment."

Wilson frowned.

Drumwright pulled out another cigar but didn't light it. "Suppose you get her and suppose you install all the equipment you have listed on paper. Who's going to drive your new toy?"

Wilson expected all kinds of arguments, but not this one. Water slapped against the dark sides of the sub in a cadence resembling music. He bristled at the term 'toy,' but he knew the admiral considered all aspects of an idea. "I really haven't thought too far in advance. I've just felt my dream and my life slipping away, trying to get something like this."

"You're young, Rick. Be patient."

"How the hell can I be patient? When I see the news, when I read the journals, I know the answers are down there.

The ocean contains knowledge, life, and healing, but nukes and missiles are more important."

"Not fair, Rick, even if there's some truth to what you're saying."

"So why discuss anything like personnel when I can't even get a boat?" He ran one hand through his hair. The wind had loosened strands from his ponytail, making them float in front of the crystal blue eyes described like ice by friends and enemies alike. His most recent girlfriend said they were like the ocean. He liked that.

Wilson pulled back his errant hair and tightened the rubber band. Long fingers gripped the railing, and he sucked in his already flat gut.

"Get a haircut and you won't have to keep pulling it back," Drumwright growled.

Wilson laughed. The admiral's hat mostly hid his bald dome. Drumwright had been an instructor during Wilson's last two years at the naval academy. He had announced his retirement off and on for the past ten years. They would have to throw his butt out of the service or carry him out on a gurney. "Unique suits me," Wilson replied.

"You'd be unique even if you were still wearing a uniform. So, who would you get to run your boat?"

"Are you saying I might have a snowball's chance in hell of even getting something like this?"

Drumwright massaged his lower back and then leaned on the railing. "I haven't put in my retirement papers yet. I think your idea of refurbishing a decommissioned boat is a damned good one. Can't figure why I didn't think of it before. Yeah, I think you can get your submarine. I have some favors to call in, too."

Wilson sucked in his breath, not daring to hope. "You mean it, Admiral?"

"Of course, I mean it! I've never BS'ed you before. I had you in my sights for a long time as a contract scientist for the Navy."

Wilson nodded. "I know you wanted me to stay in the Navy, but I wanted more freedom." He stayed in for his obligatory six years. Then he had been a scientist at several research facilities for almost twenty years. His ideas and theories formed during that time. Now he worked on his own. His few backers were getting impatient.

Drumwright grunted. "Damned straight, I wanted you to stay Navy, but it's all in the past. You get your proposal ready and I'll put a temporary restraint on this grand old girl being hauled across the harbor for the submarine recycling program. But even though she's had some of her systems stripped, you still can't hire just anyone to drive her."

Wilson had his own ideas, but he wanted to hear the admiral's thoughts first. "Who would you suggest?"

"You can't hang out a 'help wanted' sign. Can't have a tuna boat skipper in the control room."

"I won't consider retired Navy."

"I agree. They'd be too old or too worn out to care about your mission."

"Exactly. But if someone loves submarine service that much, they still wouldn't want to give up their commission for a pitiful salary. Or a terrible retirement package." Wilson sighed.

Drumwright's round face broke into a smile. "What if they remain in the service? If someone ever started a war, they could get jerked up for active service, but still have a naval retirement in the future. And…"

Wilson ground his teeth. "The Navy would have me on a leash!"

Drumwright peeled off the wrapper of his cigar.

"Those are bad for you, Admiral."

Drumwright snorted. "So's living in a tin can." He lit the cigar and puffed out the blue-gray smoke. "Rick, I don't think you'd ever be able to tell everyone to go to hell. You don't have a big enough bank account. You need the best for a project like this, and the big guns are the ones who train the best."

"So, I have to dance with the Navy and kowtow to the war department," Wilson snapped.

"To a certain extent. Homeland Security, too."

"I will not play errand boy to get a qualified crew," Wilson growled.

"You only need a few good ones at the top. Many of the sailors will be more willing to switch over. Consider, too, you won't have the same restrictions as a Navy boat."

"Captain, Executive Officer, and Chief of Boat?" Wilson suggested.

Drumwright nodded. "I think we should handpick the head of each division and let them do the recruiting. With you and me having the final say."

Wilson gaped. "You'll help me with that, too?"

Drumwright shrugged. "There are perks to being an old, fat naval desk jockey."

Wilson gazed at the submarine floating in front of him with fresh eyes. He began seeing possibilities. "I wouldn't need a full complement, since this won't be a warship. Some of the crew would be scientists."

"Not a done deal yet, Rick, but get your proposal ready. Oh, and think of where you want to park this old jalopy. We need to find a shipyard where you can work on your baby, and one that won't charge you an arm and a leg to keep her parked for at least a year."

Wilson determined it would be less than a year. "Where do I get a nuclear reactor?"

Drumwright gave a full-throated laugh now. "Amazon?" At Wilson's scowl, he coughed. "Look at government contracts. I thought you had a waterjet propulsion."

"I do, but it still relies on nuclear power to run it and they have hauled all the cells out. Not enough resources to more than plan it out on paper and in computer simulators. I'll probably need to use an old propulsion unit in the interim."

"Let's get the boat and then we can tackle the other problems," Drumwright proposed.

"Yes, sir!"

The admiral smiled around his cigar. "Wish we'd thought of this before. Would have loved seeing this beautiful beast put out to sea."

"You will, Admiral. You will."

Drumwright remained silent. Wilson glanced at him, but the older man stared at the seagulls wheeling and screeching near the pier.

"Would tomorrow morning be soon enough to bring you the proposal?" Rick asked.

"Huh? Oh, sure." The admiral knocked the cigar ash off. "Bring it by my office as soon as you're done."

"Thanks, Admiral!"

Drumwright nodded.

Wilson took one last look at the submarine, then ran to his car. Within minutes, he returned to his studio apartment, one hand booting up his computer and the other grabbing a paper and pen.

Chapter Three

Lt. Commander Lee Zuved sat ramrod straight in the restaurant booth. Not every day, a three-star admiral invited him to lunch.

Drumwright squeezed in across from him. He wheezed slightly, but still pulled out a cigar. The older man stuck it in his mouth, glaring at the server. She glared back. The admiral didn't light his cigar.

Lee wiped away his smile before the Admiral noticed. Why had the admiral invited him here? Lee had taken classes from Drumwright during his academy days and knew the man didn't do a thing without a good reason.

"What are you going to have, Commander? My treat."

"Cup of coffee will be fine, sir."

Drumwright snapped his fingers, and the server came over. "I would like your quarter pound steak burger, onion rings, and a cup of coffee, fresh. The commander will have the same." He glanced over to Lee. "Or would you rather have French Fries?"

"Uh, well. I guess French Fries, sir."

"Good."

"You'll have it in a few, gentlemen." She sauntered away.

"I imagine you want to know why I asked you to meet with me."

"Yes, sir." Understatement, thought the younger man.

"You are on the *Tulsa*, right? Executive Officer?"

Lee figured the admiral already knew that, but he answered, "A year and a half, Admiral."

"You were instrumental in the recovery of an unmanned submersible near the Puerto Rico Trench. Sent a grapple through a forward torpedo tube and snagged the submersible before it slid too far down the shelf, I understand."

"Whatever's in *Tulsa's* log, sir." Lee gave the pat answer.

"But you were on duty and you figured out how to snag it." Drumwright chomped on his cigar.

He remembered the reprimand he got from the captain. Lee had experimented, using a grapple at the end of the rod he and the chief of the boat had shoved out of the forward tube. He didn't like the idea of emulating a SEAL commando, but the 'Rube-Goldberg' device caught the rear elevation plane of the submersible. It also did damage to the tube and the bow torpedo room because there had been no way to shut the tube while they pulled the submersible out of danger. The damage rendered the boat out of commission for almost a week while making repairs. The official report stated the submarine accomplished the rescue of a valuable piece of scientific equipment. Lee said nothing.

"I haven't reached three-star without being able to read between the lines. You were also up for promotion last year."

"Standard, sir, after serving in rank...."

Drumwright waved his hand in dismissal. "Yes, yes, I know."

"Not expecting anything, sir."

"You are rather young to be a full commander."

He wished the admiral would cut to the chase. From his previous experiences with the man—not only at the academy but also at sub-school, he knew Drumwright didn't speed through anything.

Drumwright pulled out a piece of paper from his coat pocket and opened it. "Let's see. Academy with honors, especially in your major. Sub school, served on three nukes, made it to Lt. Commander by the age of thirty and then stagnant for almost four years. My ears have heard they slated you to skipper one of the new diesel class boats when they get them built. If they get them built." The admiral snorted.

Lee stiffened but said nothing. His captain mentioned he qualified for duty on a smaller submarine. It would be a way to get command and get out of the hair of a man who clearly didn't care for him. It would be a new sub, mainly doing surveillance, the minor jobs beneath the abilities of big nukes like the Los Angeles and Virginia class boats. Lee didn't know how he felt about it. One moment it felt like a demotion, another like a new opportunity, and another like it took him farther and farther from his interest in science. He even broached the subject of the new subs being used for research. Hell, they had practically laughed at him.

Drumwright brought him out of his thoughts.

"You majored in science in the academy. Why did you pick the silent service?"

"Subs fascinated me as much as science. I think there should be a way to combine the two. Also, Captain Burkhardt gave a very convincing recruitment speech."

Drumwright guffawed. "Burke always gave a convincing speech." He sobered quickly. "I noticed you checked into the progress of the new research sub Doc Wilson is refitting."

So, the admiral or someone under him checked out hits on the computer. "I didn't know those kinds of internet activities were monitored. But, yes, it would be a genuine breakthrough if someone could put together a full-sized exploration submarine and do research. I hear Doctor Wilson named it already—*Sea Dragon*? It's been used before, but it's a good name."

"Regardless, it's on the registration files," Drumwright replied.

"I understand it's hit a snag."

The admiral waved his cigar in the air. "If you are aware, even the big nukes hit snags."

The server brought their plates and coffee. "Anything else, sir?"

"We're fine, miss." Drumwright shoved his unlit cigar in his pocket. The server left. "You want to examine the *Sea Dragon*? Then you can determine for yourself if Wilson is spinning his wheels or if he really has his breakthrough."

Lee squirted ketchup on the plate and then blew on a fry. "Yes, sir. I would, but I need to report back to my boat by seventeen hundred hours."

"Lucky for you, the *Dragon's* down at the Puget Sound shipyard. Eat your lunch, Commander, then we'll take a quick drive." Drumwright squeezed mustard on his plate for the onion rings.

Lee ate some fries while they were still hot and wondered at this highly unorthodox meeting. Admiral Drumwright always had the reputation for unorthodox ideas. He had been a successful boat driver, popular with the men under him, a fantastic teacher, as well as a great lobbyist. Nothing official. Just when he thought something benefited the Navy, he grabbed on to it like a bulldog and didn't let go.

The smell of the fried onions wafted over to his side of the table and Lee wished he had let the admiral get those for him. The burger tasted good, but nerves kept him from finishing it. More than half of the meal on his plate testified to his anxiety.

"To-go box, please," Drumwright called out. The admiral had finished his meal. Nothing but a dollop of mustard remained. "We need to go. You can finish yours later. A mid-afternoon snack."

Lee wondered why the forty-plus-year naval officer hadn't retired yet. The man had to be in his seventies. Then he wondered if the new research sub had anything to do with it. "Thanks for the meal, Admiral. Let me at least lay down the tip."

"Well, I guess I can let you do that."

They strode out of the restaurant, and Drumwright motioned him to his car. "I'll have someone bring you back to get your car when we're done. I want to talk in the relative privacy of my jalopy. Sit in front."

Before him sat an older model Cadillac. When Lee opened the front door, it gave a mighty groan. He sat down, the to-go box warm on his lap. He ran his hand through his dark brown hair before putting his cap back on.

"I have read your records and remember you vaguely from sub school." Drumwright chuckled. He drove with both elbows on the steering wheel while he lit his cigar. "You got into a couple of scuffles during your academy days."

"Yes, sir. Mostly wrong assumptions about my heritage. I look Native American, but I'm eastern European. And no fights since then."

"I know."

"Admiral, permission to speak freely?"

"Go ahead, Commander."

"What the hell is all this about?"

"I would like to wait to answer your question, my boy. Until you've seen the boat."

Something more than curiosity about his past triggered Drumwright's interest.

"So, what have you found out about this project?" Drumwright asked.

"Not much, sir, despite the curiosity surrounding it. It surprised me when the Navy sold the boat to Dr. Wilson."

"Do you think the Navy should have sold a former ballistic nuke to a scientist?"

"I can't make a judgement as to the abilities of Dr. Wilson to convert something that massive. But I agree the LA's are damned fine boats to just be cut to scrap."

"I agree with you, Commander. To Wilson's credit, he didn't explode when they attached a few strings to the sale. He just smoldered."

There were several minutes of silence, each man to his own thoughts.

Chapter Four

They neared the Puget Sound shipyard. Several ships waited in dry dock in various stages of repair. Then he saw a submarine. It looked like any other LA class boat, but as they drove closer, Lee could see differences.

Mainly, he noticed open spaces. "Do you know what's taking the place of the missiles, sir?"

Drumwright parked. "I believe Rick is dividing the area into research pods. He's got lots of ideas but understands the reality of the space he's inherited."

Lee nodded. The substantial change would have to be inside. The submarine no longer served as a war machine. He felt the power of the boat's history and the men who had served her.

"Let's go aboard. No officer of the deck since this is a decommissioned vessel."

"Doesn't Dr. Wilson keep any guards?"

The admiral chuckled. "There's people here." He pointed to a figure up on the sail. "My people. Wilson spends most of his time dreaming, planning, and putting his new baby together."

A tall, burly, dark-skinned man stood guard on the sail of the submarine. Lee guessed this man had been a Chief Petty Officer—maybe even a Chief of the Boat. Yes, definitely a COB. He wore standard camo fatigues and held a set of binoculars in one hand. A pistol was holstered on his hip. The man peered at him, but Lee passed muster by his association with the admiral.

"Keeping out the riff-raff, Bates?" Drumwright asked.

"Trying to, sir. Haven't had to toss anyone in the bay yet." Bates had a deep-from-the-diaphragm laugh.

He addressed Bates, who acted as the Officer of the Deck. "Commander Lee Zuved, coming to see Dr. Wilson."

"Welcome aboard, Commander."

"Thanks, Chief."

Bates grinned. "How'd you know, sir?"

Lee returned the smile. "You have the Chief Petty Officer look."

"I'll let Dr. Wilson know you are here."

Drumwright shook his head. "I'll introduce Commander Zuved when we get down there."

"Aye, aye, sir."

"After you, Commander."

Lee climbed through the bridge cockpit and down to the control room. The absence of electronic and surveillance noises disconcerted him. One of the partially bare walls made the room appear spacious. Newly installed computers lined the other wall, more streamlined than the originals and quieter.

"Welcome aboard, Admiral." A dark-haired young man in jeans and a tee-shirt greeted them.

"Thanks, Corry. This is Commander Zuved from the *Tulsa.*"

The man reached out to shake Zuved's hand. "I'm Corry Ikeda, the head computer tech for this project." Corry pointed in front of him. "Doc's that way."

Beyond the control room, Lee and Drumwright found Dr. Wilson. He straddled something appearing similar to a torpedo, but with differences. The metal nose peeled open like the petals of a flower. A rod shot out, landing on the floor with a clang. The end contained something resembling a prosthetic hand. It opened, then closed. Wilson cursed, but it didn't open again.

Lee recognized it—a remote rescue system similar to what he had jury-rigged a year ago—except he didn't have a prosthetic hand. So, someone *had* paid attention, but Wilson's efforts were unsuccessful. The idea the scientist felt this contraption had merit gratified Lee.

Drumwright stayed uncharacteristically quiet. "Perhaps it would be more successful with a grappling-style hook, depending on the aim of the shooter. Maybe a magnet for metal objects."

Wilson jerked up in surprise. "Don't sneak up on me like that!" He frowned at the admiral. "I thought I told you I didn't want any of your…"

"My boy, don't bite the hand feeding you, so to speak."

Wilson glared at Lee. The commander stood stiffly but said nothing.

"Just so happens this is the man who gave you the idea for this contraption. Jury-rigged, but it saved a very costly submersible."

"Lee Zuved, Doctor. I serve as executive officer on the *Tulsa*." He held out his hand. Wilson took it.

"Under Marcum Skoren? My condolences, sir." He glanced at Lee's insignia. "Commander, welcome aboard."

He ignored the jibe at his commanding officer, refusing to indulge in gossip. "Renaming her *Sea Dragon*?"

"I know the Chinese have, or had, a vessel of the same name, and so have we, but I think it's going to fit." Wilson's eyes darted to Drumwright and then back to Lee. "Why are you here?"

"The admiral asked me if I wanted to see your boat and I said yes."

Drumwright finally spoke up. "Commander Zuved has also been keeping up with your progress."

Lee frowned, feeling such information to be his own business.

"I don't think you could do better to get Commander Zuved as your boat driver," Drumwright stated.

"What?" Lee and Wilson said at the same time.

"I'm not old enough to retire," he said, still surprised.

Drumwright laughed. "You wouldn't be retired. Navy has a small chunk of this boat, as I figured they would. They are requiring—rather demanding the command team be at least reserve naval officers. I'm trying to keep you on active status."

"Commander Zuved? Scuttlebutt says you're slated for one of those non-nuke boats supposedly being built," Wilson added.

Were there any secrets? "Supposedly." Lee steered the conversation away from that touchy subject. "How long will it be before her launch?"

"A year," Drumwright replied. "Long enough for you to be promoted to full commander."

He snorted. "I think hell will freeze over first."

"You're eligible, son. Lot of the captains are retiring. Some are getting promoted. Young blood coming up."

"Do I get a say in this?" Wilson asked, wiping greasy hands on a towel.

"Of course," Drumwright replied.

Wilson looked Lee up and down for a moment. "Are you interested, Commander? Just to warn you, I am irascible, impatient..."

Drumwright harrumphed. "Rick…"

"Okay, I am impatient with incompetents all the time. Impatient with progress a lot; it's never fast enough, but I know the virtues of meticulous study. I will be on the boat for all of her missions…"

"When not being forced to politic," Drumwright added.

"Kissing the feet of others. I need to get this project out of dry dock," Wilson snapped.

"Commander Zuved's major field at the academy included science," Drumwright interjected.

"Oh? Why did you go into submarine school then?"

"Equal love. I felt I could get more of both worlds in a sub."

Wilson nodded. "Well, for what it's worth, I *will* be here on most missions. If you choose to take this position, I will leave boat operations to you and whoever the executive officer ends up being."

The job interested him. Very much. "Yes, I would like to skipper your boat, but I also want my back door left open. Knowing how fickle the government is."

Wilson nodded. "I don't think we need to publicize this right now. I'm also looking for a good Executive Officer. If you have any suggestions for an XO, I'll consider them." He paused, rubbing his chin. "I also want to leave my back door open, so you won't be insulted if I do a background check, will you?"

Drumwright handed the scientist a manila envelope. "Here, this should have everything."

No surprise to Lee. "We will also need a good Chief of Boat, as well."

Wilson rolled the envelope up and shoved it into his back pocket. "Haven't worked really hard on personnel yet. I know who I'm going to approach for the scientific crew, but I'll give you and the admiral free rein on the command crew."

"They'll have to be cleared, Doctor."

Wilson waved his hand and then pushed some of his errant hair out of his eyes. "Of course."

Lee gazed around at the open spaces. "How much input would I have on refit, Doctor?"

"I'll take any suggestions under consideration," Wilson replied.

Drumwright cleared his throat. "Commander, I will be liaison between your current assignment and this boat. Keep a low profile for now."

"Of course, and I understand." Lee turned to Dr. Wilson. "I look forward to working with you."

Wilson chuckled. "With some of the hoops I have to jump through, I wouldn't hold my breath for it to happen soon."

"Hopefully, in a year, she'll be ready."

"You have a spare nuclear reactor in your pocket?" Wilson asked.

He grinned. "No. The admiral will have to help you with that."

"By damn, I'll get one," Drumwright thundered. "Keep your shirt on!"

Lee glanced at his watch. "I hope you gentlemen will excuse me. I would love to look over the entire sub, but I don't want to be late reporting to *my* boat."

"Glad to meet you, Commander."

"You, too, Doctor. By the way, I have someone in mind for an executive officer, but I need to talk to him privately first. You trust me?"

Wilson nodded. "Feel free, just so long as I don't start seeing headlines in the papers."

"You won't."

"I need to get back to work requisitioning a nuclear reactor," the admiral said. "I'll drive you back to your car, Commander."

"Yes, sir. Thanks." As he climbed back up the sail ladder, he felt lighter of heart than he had at the beginning of the day. Lee stood on the bridge for a moment. The planes stuck out like eagles' wings. His own boat. His own command! Could he do it? He knew from rumor Wilson involved himself deeply in all of his projects, but Drumwright seemed capable of bringing the scientist down to Earth. And then Lee remembered the man's promise to leave the driving to him. He believed he would.

"Second thoughts, Commander?"

"Only about my ability to do the job."

"I wouldn't have brought you here if I didn't think you were capable."

"Thanks, Admiral."

Drumwright relit his cigar. "I will keep you up on everything happening with *Sea Dragon*. You go chasing off after your ideal executive officer."

"Yes, sir!"

Chapter Five

Lieutenant Commander Guion Macon, the highest ranking black officer on the submarine, *Chattanooga*, gazed at the note in his hand. He hadn't heard from his friend, Lee Zuved, for half a year, about the time they got together to celebrate Macon's position as an executive officer. They had toasted, swapped stories, and enjoyed themselves thoroughly. Macon could tell life had been tense for his friend, but Lee didn't gripe. Macon chose not to pry.

The note included an invitation for dinner and drinks. Lee must have checked his boat's schedule. Macon looked in the tiny mirror. His dark brown face and hazel eyes, along with his well-toned body, were ready for a night on the town with his best academy buddy.

Walking to Communications, Macon responded to the note.

***

Two weeks later, Macon scowled at the sign softly glowing in front of him. *Lee picks an exclusive club to have dinner and drinks?*

As he approached the door, a rotund, middle-aged man in a fancy red and gold uniform stepped in front of him. "Do you have a reservation, sir?"

"I came by invitation."

"Under what name?"

"Zuved."

"Yes, sir. Zuved and Drumwright. Please follow me."

Drumwright? He recognized the name. What would a three-star want with him and Lee?

The man opened the door and motioned him ahead. Inside, the doorman pointed toward a small room. When Macon walked through the narrow doorway, he saw Lee alone at a table. Sliding into an elegant, richly upholstered seat opposite his friend and fellow submariner, the years since the academy seemed to melt away. They did every time they got together.

"Lee, did you forget my basic requirements for a good time?"

"Nope, I remember. Loud music, beautiful dates, and decent food. Had something else in mind for tonight."

"What?"

Lee leaned over the table. "Mace?"

Macon's friends called him Mace. Macon always thought it hilarious to be named after a black astronaut and he ended up 'twenty thousand leagues under the sea.' He brought his mind back to his friend. This became more cloak and dagger. "Come on, Lee. What's up?"

His friend had a Cheshire cat smile. "I have been offered my own command."

Macon brightened and then slapped Lee on the shoulder. "What's the name of the lucky boat?"

"Sea Dragon."

Macon ran a three-second mental search. "Never heard of it."

"Because she's not finished yet. Refitting a Los Angeles submarine."

"They all have names of cities, except the *Rickover*. And refitting rarely entails a renaming." Macon's curiosity jumped into the stratosphere.

"This one does. Being totally refitted for research missions."

Lee had accepted captaincy on Wilson's Folly? He asked.

"I have indeed."

"Why did you agree to serve on a research boat?"

Lee held up his hand as a server brought in drinks. "I ordered before you got here."

"Thanks." Macon waited. Lee rarely did anything without a good reason.

Lee took a sip of his drink before continuing. "The navy slated me for one of the modern diesels, but who knows if the Navy will ever build those."

"I hear they will be much better than the old diesel pig boats."

"I can't help but picture shore watching and being a glorified errand boy."

"Lee, you think it'll be like a demotion?"

"Stupid, but yeah. That's what it feels like and they haven't even gotten them off the drawing board yet."

"Understandable, though." Macon took a sip of his drink. A perfectly dry martini. "So what makes this pig in a poke so appealing?"

"It'll be research. Not one ICBM in the entire boat."

"No missiles? Defenseless?"

"No, there will be a half-dozen non-nuclear warhead torpedoes. Enough to scare off all but the most determined bad guys." Lee took a sip of his drink, white wine in an elegant wine glass. "Besides, you know I majored in marine biology at the academy."

"Yeah, with a side of chemistry," Mace said. "You always were an over-achiever. Surprised you had time to delve into subs."

Lee laughed. "I saw the boat when they offered me the job. Wilson may be bellicose, but I saw what he's attempting to do, and it excited me."

"I repeat, what does this do to your commission? You haven't had enough time for a full retirement."

"Navy has a little influence here. Wilson has to have experienced sub drivers in charge and he won't accept a retiree as the captain."

Mace could feel Lee's excitement. "So, you'll skipper this boat with your commission and active status?"

Lee took a deep breath. "That's what Drumwright's trying to do, but I'd take it on reserve status."

"You want it bad."

"Yes, but this is not official yet."

"You mean your skipper doesn't know?"

"One or two more hurdles and then we can make assignments," Lee said, shaking his head.

Mace studied his friend and then his half empty—or half full—glass. "You didn't invite me here to celebrate."

"Not exactly. I want you to be a plank owner of *Sea Dragon* as my XO. I want you at my back."

Macon said nothing for several minutes. He picked up and put down his glass a few times. "I need some time to think, Lee." His current naval assignment gave him great security. A few more years and he'd be eligible for his own boat.

"This isn't an official posting, Mace. Ask questions. Think about it. Pray; whatever you need to do. And if you say no, I'll understand."

"You trying to dissuade me?"

"No, no. I just don't…."

Macon chuckled. "Helluva good skipper you'll be. Worried about what everyone thinks."

"No, only what you think. We were a team at the academy." Lee smiled. "To the academy." They clinked their glasses together.

"To the ocean, the Navy, and what we still have to learn," Macon said. He wouldn't mind an XO posting under Lee Zuved. His friend possessed the ability to be a topnotch boat driver.

"Sounds to me like you are interested in the job," a deep voice broke into his reverie.

Mace saw who approached and stood up. Drumwright motioned him back down and sat next to him. "I thought you were at the head of the line when I told Commander Zuved to consider an excellent executive officer."

"Admiral, can I assume you are backing this venture?"

"I wholeheartedly back it, but mostly in a behind-the-scenes capacity." He motioned to the server and ordered a beer. He pulled out a cigar—but didn't light it. When the server brought his drink, a frown told volumes.

"Not going to light it, young man. Even admirals know how to follow orders."

The server smiled. "Ready to order, gentlemen?"

Drumwright waved him off. "Give us a few more minutes. About ten."

"Yes, sir."

"Bring some chips and dip," Lee said. "Some of your fancy spinach and crab dip."

"Yes, sir. It will be right out."

Drumwright paused until the man walked away from the table. "No pressure, but what are your feelings, Commander Macon?"

"I have a few questions you might answer, sir."

"Shoot."

"This isn't a Navy ship. This is a privately owned vessel."

"But Dr. Wilson is not privately wealthy," Drumwright interjected. "Although he bought the boat, he couldn't afford all the hardware. The Navy has an interest in this."

"So, Admiral, would I have to give up my commission?"

"Considering you are shy a few years for a full retirement, it's a viable question. The short answer is no; you'd still hold rank, you'd still be Navy and get Navy pay. The Navy, and indeed, Dr. Wilson, were worried about something this sophisticated and large in the hands of a fishing scow skipper."

Mace nodded. "So, the government insisted on qualified sub-drivers."

The server reappeared with the appetizers. Drumwright again said nothing until he left.

"That became part of the deal, Commander. The navy agreed to sell something they normally scrap but made stipulations about who would be in charge of day-to-day operations. Wilson already understood he needed qualified personnel. And he wanted people young enough to take the job and run with it."

"Okay, Admiral, let's say I'm interested. I like the idea of working with Commander Zuved, and I'm flattered by his interest in my services. I am intrigued about working on a nuke, but without the feeling of looking for a fight. But…"

"But you aren't sure about working with a civilian, probably more than just the one."

"I think even with full Navy, it would be a unique experience."

"But not insurmountable, I hope," Drumwright said.

"No, not insurmountable," Macon responded. "Who besides us would be Navy, sir?"

The server returned, and the three men glanced over their menus. Macon decided and placed his order. The other two men did the same.

"Definitely senior officers. About ten. Heads of departments mainly, as well as Chief of Boat. I think civilians who did shorter stints in the Navy and some retirees who are still fit can fill a lot of the lower positions," Drumwright continued.

Macon revisited a previous question. "What's the long answer, Admiral, or is there one?"

Drumwright paused for a moment. "Ah, status and pay. I am still negotiating, but I think part of the time you'd be reserve. But as long as you're serving, you'll be getting the same pay. However, Wilson doesn't want you to be totally under the thumb of the Pentagon. He doesn't want them calling up reservists for minor skirmishes and leaving *Dragon* at the dock. Can't say as I blame him, since the efficiency of a vessel depends on the personnel serving her. If you have your people getting jerked around on other assignments at the drop of a hat, morale plummets. Still, Warren Buffet wouldn't be able to put together something of this scope without help, so we've made concessions—hence the reserve status."

"I guess Wilson's primary concern might be if the Navy told him to do something covert. Like a spy mission or something similar," Mace mused.

Drumwright nodded. "Exactly, and I have every intention of nipping that idea in the bud. You interested?"

Mace glanced at Lee, whose face remained inscrutable behind his glass. Macon turned back to the admiral. "I believe I am."

"To the silent service, regardless of the mission." Drumwright raised his glass and the three men toasted submariners everywhere.

Chapter Six

"What in the world are these televisions going to be used for?" Lee stood in *Sea Dragon's* refurbished control room, watching as medium-sized flat screen monitors were fastened to the wall, three in the bow section and three in the aft. The techs' ability to fit them in with all the other electronics needed to run a submarine of this size amazed him.

"Pretty slick, eh?" Wilson asked.

"I guess, if I knew their purpose."

"One thing I have been working on is the ability for a submarine to actually see what's out there. Not hear, but also see."

"You mean those will show us what's outside? Like a window would?" Lee felt like he asked silly questions—since outside cameras just weren't viable to put on a big submarine.

Wilson nodded, his ponytail bobbing.

"How will they do it? I mean, cameras have been unfeasible in the past."

"I know. But these aren't regular cameras attached to the hull. Fiber optics can reveal objects in small and confined spaces, and a similar technology could show us the world in real time. Anyway, I have been experimenting over the years and I developed a fiber that can be formed in a flat shape."

"And you incorporated it into the hull?" Lee asked.

"Indeed, I have. Let me show you with the auxiliary power source." Wilson turned on a smallish box hooked to his belt and then turned on one monitor. At first it showed nothing. Wilson sat down in a narrow seat and typed into the laptop sitting below the screen. Shadowy shapes focused and showed Lee the ocean floor.

The skipper gasped. He knew he saw the area below the *Dragon*. Debris covered with silt, small marine animals, and an occasional fish appeared and then disappeared.

Wilson typed in more commands, and Lee saw the flickering light mix with the shadows. This monitor showed the area ahead of the bow. The wake of a small boat wavered the pictures coming on the screen, but they showed up amazingly sharp.

"I'll be damned," he murmured. "And it will be just as sharp when we're underway?"

"Theoretically. We'll test it and find out."

"And I've been meaning to ask how you managed Virginia-class propulsion unit on our beautiful boat. Which senator did you have to blackmail?"

Doc laughed. "I didn't. I put in my wish list and the admiral drew in favors or twisted arms—perhaps both."

Lee shook his head. Having a water-jet style of propulsion would eliminate the noise—and wear and tear a propeller shaft would create. He couldn't wait until he could lay his transfer papers on Captain Skoren's desk. It really would get awkward if it didn't happen soon.

"I think you're going to need to let your commander know about your intentions quickly," Wilson said, as though reading his mind.

"Just waiting for the admiral to give me the go-ahead."

Wilson said nothing as he worked on his computer.

"Since the top positions are a secret, we can't reach out to many eligible officers and sailors." Lee looked up and saw the admiral.

"No problem, gentlemen," boomed Drumwright.

"Welcome aboard, Admiral. And why is it no problem?"

"You are transferring ASAP and then taking two months of the vacation you've accrued. So's your new exec."

"I have that much?" Lee asked.

"You've lost a little vacation time each year, Lee," Drumwright replied. "Put it to use this year. Do what you're doing now. Help get this beautiful boat ready to sail!"

He grinned. "Aye, aye, Admiral." He turned back to Wilson.

"No, not tomorrow. Get your butt off the boat and deliver the news to Captain Skoren. It might be helpful to tell him before he gets the paperwork. It's on its way."

"What?" Lee felt the blood drain to his toes. He had always looked forward to transferring, but actually talking to his commanding officer about the same?

"Get the hell out of here. Now!"

He almost saluted. "Gone!" He heard laughter following him off the boat.

Commander Skoren took it well. When Lee took his leave of the boat, the men wished him good luck. Several asked about his new assignment. Most gawked when he told them, and a few asked if there might be room for them. Skoren wouldn't mind his leaving, but he'd sure be boiling if Lee took sailors and junior officers with him. He suggested they email him.

Chapter Seven

Terrill Bates hung out on the sail of the *Sea Dragon*. He watched the sun lower toward the horizon, tinging the bottoms of the wispy clouds. Only Doc Wilson still worked below. Bates sniffed the odor of saltwater, dead fish, oil, and human refuse. While not as pleasant as being out to sea, he had become accustomed to it. This security job had lasted the most part of the past year—not paying much, but he wouldn't have traded it for any fancy bank or business security positions.

Watching the resurrection of this magnificent vessel had been well worth it. Now it would be over soon. The installation of most of the new systems was completed. The boat had a skipper and an executive officer and most of her department heads.

"Twenty assassins could have snuck on board," Doc called as he climbed through the hatch.

Bates jumped half a foot. "Oh, Doc. Sorry, sir. Just thinking."

Doc leaned against the railing, surveying the length of the submarine. "She's beautiful."

"Yes, sir. She is."

"What are your plans after we sail?"

Bates looked down at his dark hands grasping the rail of his second home. "I don't know. Another security job somewhere, I guess."

"I can give you a recommendation. If that's what you really want."

"I'd appreciate it." Then he paused. *What do I really want? No, dammit, the only recommendation I want is to work on this beautiful submarine.*

"Did you have a favorite ship? You were on several, weren't you?"

Bates thought a bit. He had joined the Navy in the glory years of the LA class submarines and had trained on one. He'd served on nukes—like this one. "*Salt Lake City.*"

Wilson glanced over at him. "Ah, so you are already familiar with LA class boats."

Bates nodded. "Did a stint on a surface ship after *Salt Lake City.*"

"How did you like it?"

Bates laughed. "Felt like I could easily slide over the rail and end up in the water."

Doc laughed with him. "So, you like subs better?"

"You bet!" A seagull landed on a guy wire nearby. This seagull showed up every day to mooch crumbs or leftovers. He pulled a half a cookie from lunch and tossed it to the beggar. The gull flapped upward and snatched the treat in mid-air.

The bird swooped to a secure place to eat his meal as several other gulls flew in to grab a bite.

"Terrill, you thought about serving on the *Dragon*?"

Bates stared at his boss for a long moment before replying. "Of course, I've thought of it, but didn't know I had a chance at something like this."

"Why not?"

"I thought Zuved and Macon were calling the shots."

"Admiral Drumwright said Zuved had you pegged right away as a chief petty officer."

"So, who's the Chief of Boat?"

"We don't have a COB yet. I told 'em to give me their ideas before they asked anyone."

Bates remained quiet.

"The captain suggested you. Macon agreed." Doc turned to him. "I received no other suggestions. No need. I want you."

Bates gaped at him. "Chief of *this* boat? The *Dragon*?"

Doc nodded. "If you want it."

It took about five seconds for his brain to process the conversation, and then he whooped, sending the squawking gulls skyward.

***

Bates sang all the way home and only stopped singing when he kissed his wife, Andrea. She laughed and kissed him back. The kids looked up from the TV show they were watching. Sometimes, since he had become security guard for the submarine, he came home after Tessa and Terrill, jr. had gone to bed.

"I have an announcement to make!" he shouted over the television. To her credit, Tessa only did a small eye roll and then put the TV on mute.

Andrea leaned her head on her husband's arm and murmured, "I've got a pretty good idea, but I'd rather hear it aloud from you."

"They have selected me to be the Chief of the Boat. I'll be COB of *Sea Dragon*."

Terry's eyes grew large. "The submarine you've been working on, Dad?"

Terrill nodded, then glanced at Andrea. "Did you know?"

She nodded. "Admiral Drumwright called, asking how I felt about you joining the crew of *Sea Dragon*. Made me ecstatic, of course. I know you've missed the Navy these past few years. I've missed it even longer." Andrea turned to the kids, a mysterious gleam in her eye. "I need to ask you two a question."

Terry, the fourteen-year-old, climbed up on the back of the couch, his long legs dangling to the floor. Tessa, their oldest at sixteen, lounged over the top. "What's up, Mom? You have the same look Scooter has when he's slipped out and caught a mouse or something."

"You remember Admiral Drumwright, don't you?"

"Sure," Terry replied. "The old white guy who came by last month. He stuck his cigar in his pocket."

Bates hid his smile.

"Yes, he's the one," Andrea said. "When he called, he asked if I might be interested in taking a position on the *Sea Dragon*."

"Whoa!" Terry said. "Seriously?"

"What?" Tessa blurted out. "What are we going to do? Jeez! Did you forget about us?"

Andrea frowned, then brightened. "Your Grampa and Gram would be delighted to come and stay here while we go out. Your dad and I wouldn't always go out together, either."

"You sure you want to do this?" Tessa blinked, trying to hold back tears.

"I think you two are old enough for us to be gone on missions. These assignments won't be as long as a regular navy submarine voyage."

"Have you been on a submarine?" Terry's eyes shone with excitement.

"I trained to work on submarines, but I had your sister before they assigned female petty officers to submarines. I served on surface vessels." She turned to their daughter. "Is that what you're worried about? Safety?" Andrea asked.

"I don't know, Mom. I love Gram and Grampa, but you'd be gone so long and…." She stopped.

Terrill saw a tear slide down his daughter's face.

"I think we need to have a council," Bates said, hugging his daughter. "Your choice for the place, Tessa."

"Here's fine." They all squeezed on the couch, pushing the cat off. The cat climbed on Tessa's lap. She hugged the animal so tightly the cat squirmed. "Why do you want to leave us?"

Andrea wrapped her arm around her daughter's shoulders. "I don't want to *leave* you. I'm not abandoning you. It's just this is such a great opportunity."

"You have a job. In the tax office."

"Sometimes I dream all of those forms are some kind of ocean or lake and I'm drowning in them."

"Sounds more like a nightmare," Terry quipped.

"It is," Andrea murmured. "A never-ending nightmare."

"What would you be doing on a submarine better than a safe accountant job?" Tessa asked.

"On April 15th, sometimes a tax office isn't safe. But I was a darned good supply officer in the Navy."

Tessa looked sideways at Andrea and rolled her eyes. "Supply officer? You mean ordering food and underwear?"

Andrea laughed. "My last duty station, I ordered all the food supplies, and the shipboard supplies, some of which I won't mention. And yes, I did order personal supplies if sailors needed them. I got them fast, and I got the correct items at over a ninety-eight percent efficiency."

"Your mother got awards for her efficiency," Terrill bragged. "I might add I'm being offered a higher pay raise with better benefits than I am getting at my security job. So's your mom."

"But when we have a concert?" Tessa asked. "Or a game? Or a birthday?"

Andrea sighed. "That's the tough part, but Gram and Grandpa would be there for you and send the video links to us. I know it would not be the same thing as us being there. As to birthdays, we'll work it out so at least one of us will have leave."

Terrill knew his wife struggled with her emotions, just as their daughter did. "Which classes do you do best in at school?"

"ROTC!" Terry said immediately.

"Zoology," Tessa answered more slowly.

"Why?"

"I've told you before, Mom. Because zoology is interesting. I hope I can get a job at an aquarium or a zoo when I graduate next year. I want to help animals."

Terrill said nothing. Neither did his wife. He could see the wheels turning inside their heads.

"You want to work on a submarine because it's interesting." Tessa finally said.

Andrea took a deep breath. "When I served on ships, I felt like I did something useful. But on *Sea Dragon*, it would be more. *Sea Dragon* is doing something useful for everyone. I'll be ordering supplies, which most people would see as boring, but helping everyone do a job to help our planet and people."

"I think I understand, Mom," Terry admitted.

Tessa hugged her mother. "I guess I do, too. Will you be able to call us?"

Terrill nodded. "Modern military submarines would be under tight restrictions, but there won't be as many rules with *Sea Dragon*. So we can call you more often."

Tessa still looked concerned. "Can we do a trial run?"

Andrea nodded. "How about we give it a year and if it doesn't work out for you two, then I will quit."

"A year is a lifetime. How about six months?"

"You told me the other day, you couldn't believe how fast your sophomore year went."

Tessa sighed. "Okay. We can try a year."

The next day, Andrea accepted a post on *Sea Dragon*.

Chapter Eight

Six months later, *Sea Dragon's* complement had to borrow Bremerton's convention center for everyone to meet in. Wilson and Drumwright allowed no press at this meeting. It pleased Lee, too, since he figured there'd be plenty of 'what if' questions from the scientists about life on a submarine.

He, Drumwright, Wilson, Macon, and Chief Petty Officer Bates sat at a table in front of the assembled group. In the first row, sat Lieutenant Thom Davis, head Navigational officer, Lieutenant Frank Lopez, the nuclear reactor/engines officer, Ensign Eric Meyers, their chief medical officer, and Chief Andrea Bates, head of supply. Lee had seen the roster for each division and it impressed him. All were highly qualified personnel. He hoped the admiral worked his magic with their reserve status, too. Others were civilians qualified to do specific jobs. They had assured him working and living in a submarine wouldn't bother them. It would be interesting to see if any bailed at the end of this relatively short mission.

Lee knew the scientists were also qualified—Wilson had hand-picked everyone, even down to the few apprentices he insisted needed to be aboard. There were almost two dozen scientists with specialties from marine archaeology to climatology.

Everyone had been briefed privately, but a few questions always surfaced when individuals got together in a group this big.

The inevitable first one came from a middle-aged scientist, Dr. Wendy Scherer. "I've been told space is tight on a submarine. Will we all be sharing bunks or hammocks in one extensive area?"

"We're sharing rooms, Dr. Scherer, not bunks. Since we reconfigured some parts of the boat, there are small, partitioned rooms for the ladies—three in a cabin. There are separate areas where our young men will bunk."

"Thank you, Captain Zuved."

"How fast does the ship go?"

Another inevitable question. "By tradition, we often refer to submarines as boats. Regardless, our fastest speed averages thirty-five miles per hour. We'll get to Hawaii in about four to five days."

The instructions and questions only lasted an hour. By then, the catering company had brought dinner, and the group adjourned to enjoy an excellent meal.

***

Lee stood on the pier gazing at the seventy-strong complement standing in lines of ten men and women, seven deep. Some were older, having come out of retirement, but most of these starry-eyed folks were his age or younger.

Admiral Drumwright stood next to him and Doc Wilson was next to the admiral. Commander Macon, executive officer of the boat, stood steel-rod straight on Lee's left. Terrill Bates, the Chief of Boat, stood next to Macon. Press helicopters thrummed above them. Two escort tugs waited out in the harbor.

"My friends," Drumwright began, "you are the beginning of a new era at sea." The admiral sounded a little out of breath. He had lost a great deal of weight over the past six months and looked sallow. "You have all been hand-picked for this submarine. When you step aboard *Sea Dragon*, realize she already had a grand life as a sentinel for our country. Now you are entering a vessel working for the world." There were loud cheers.

Wilson continued, "We are going to discover things only the science fiction writers could imagine. Probably couldn't imagine. You are already familiar with your duties, your stations, and the protocol of something new like this. *Dragon*, formerly an attack submarine, has been retrofitted with advanced propulsion and reinforced hull, enabling it to reach greater depths than a typical LA class submarine. When we need to, we have a mini-vehicle to go even deeper. There is more room for science stations. If we are successful, it's possible there may be a fleet of similar submarines and surface vessels."

"Welcome aboard, ladies and gentlemen!" Drumwright ended. The cheers were thunderous.

The press stood behind the complement, capturing the entire event. Lee congratulated Wilson for requiring a short send-off.

Doc Wilson motioned to the boat, sitting in silent splendor. Lee and Macon stepped on the gangplank, with Doc following. The two executive officers welcomed the crew all-aboard from the Chief Medical Officer to the cook. Although everyone had already been on *Sea Dragon*, they stood a moment before going below.

"Mr. Macon," Lee ordered his XO, "prepare to get under way."

"Aye, aye, sir," Mace replied formally.

Two members of the press accompanied the boat out of the sound, and they gawked and took pictures before stepping aboard. Lee pulled in a breath of sea air, reveling in the tang of salt, fish, and the slight smell of detritus always accompanying human presence.

Lee followed Wilson up to the bridge, the tiny deck at the top of the sail. While the scientist climbed below, he watched as they cast the lines off. He waved to the admiral still standing on the dock. Drumwright successfully bent arms in the back rooms of every place from the Naval office to the Oval office. Now these explorers had the responsibility to make this dream work.

The admiral waved back. He shouted, "Let's see this lady sail!"

Lee saluted and shouted back, "Aye, aye, sir!" He gave orders for the sub to get underway. *Sea Dragon* slid out of her dock smoothly.

The communicator called the all clear, and the submarine headed for the open ocean.

Drumwright walked to the end of the pier, watching them. He waved again. Two tugs stood off the bow, but Wilson insisted *Sea Dragon* would leave under her own power.

"Take her out, quarter speed," Lee ordered.

Admiral Drumwright stood alone, lonely, despite the gaggle of press, small puffs of smoke curling above his head. Soon Drumwright and the dock disappeared out of sight. Still, the captain stood on the bridge with the officer of the deck, the salt breeze pulling at his hat. He took it off and let the sea air dry his sweaty brow. They were well beyond the entrance of the sound and still he stood there.

Chapter Nine

"Captain, we are ready to dive anytime you order." Mace sounded eager on the communicator.

"I'll be right below." Lee nodded to the officer of the deck, a young lieutenant from his previous assignment.

He took one last look around him—at the tall, oval shaft of the sail, with her bow planes spreading out like eagle's wings. Farther below, the water sluiced over the bow. Then he climbed down the ladder to the control room. Lt. Trent followed, closing the hatches behind them. People sat at the computers and controls, but after a glance, Lee studied the large monitors mounted above the duty stations.

He loved this updated technology, letting them actually see almost every inch of the hull and the ocean beyond, farther than windows would. They cruised just below the surface until they were out of the sound and into the Pacific.

"Ahead, one quarter. Down bubble. Cruise depth one hundred feet," Macon ordered.

Lee felt the slight shift as the sub slid smoothly into its new position. The monitors picked up the ocean floor with its human footprint scattered in sloppy array. Tires, disintegrating planks, even the mud-covered shape of a sunken boat. Sailboat, most likely. As they sailed further, the ocean floor fell away, but the human factor remained—limited ocean flora and little fauna.

"Disgusting," Wilson muttered beside him.

Lee nodded. "We'll see how much pollution has encroached around the Hawaiian Islands." Their first voyage and assignment required them to visit various islands tracking any anomalies. Their information would go into a database where scientists could determine whether it was climate change. They also were to record conservation efforts on the reefs and sea shelves. Doc Wilson had assembled several teams, allowing studies to take place simultaneously. This would verify the abilities of a research sub like *Sea Dragon*.

"Skipper, I have a message for you from communications," came a young voice.

Lee waited for the skipper to answer. Then he realized he was the skipper. Lee felt his cheeks warm as he turned toward the young man holding the iPad. With a nod, he took the device and scanned the message with a smile. It came from Drumwright.

'You made it! Congratulations!'

"This is for you, too, Doc," Lee said, handing the computer to Wilson.

His boss looked at it, and he, too, grinned. "We have to prove ourselves now," he said, his eyes shining in excitement.

Lee typed *'thanks, wish you were here'* and handed the device back to the sailor.

Another crewmember approached him with a chart. "Your approval on the room assignments, Captain." Lee studied the names, also noting their room assignments. The term 'room' stretched the definition of a room. They were partitioned areas with several bunks each, a fold down desk, a small rod in a cubby for clothes, and a mirror. The submarine's refit included accommodations for scientists and female crewmembers. "Looks in order, but have someone check with the individuals and make sure they are as comfortable as they can be. Until we get to Hawaii, we can't make any changes other than swapping roomies."

"Aye, sir."

"Glad we had the bit of room to make those changes," Doc commented.

"So am I." Most of the room left by the removal of the ballistic missiles had been converted to laboratories and science stations. Doc even had a few tanks installed for specimens. Most of the systems running the *Dragon* remained the same or at least in the same spaces. The propulsion system switched to the new pump-jet or hydro-jet system. How the doctor and Admiral Drumwright managed such a miracle, he didn't know, but Lee looked forward to the quieter ride. "Do we have a home base yet?"

Doc sighed. "Still waiting for final approval from the Alaskan government, but I think so. Juneau figures they'll get some tourist benefit out of us or something."

Lee chuckled softly. "They might. I doubt they get many civilian LA class submarines up there."

Doc laughed with him. "I just wish we could have gotten something in the lower forty-eight."

"Except for a few times a year, Juneau will be better than the West coast. The only problem is the logistics of getting the crewmembers home."

"That's what I am talking about. And for those who want to live up there, the cost-of-living stinks."

Lee mused. "Why does it have to be a U.S. mainland base?"

"What do you mean?"

"What about Hawaii? We're going there. Maybe we could work something out with the Hawaiian government."

"Their cost of living is high, too."

"We'll figure something out," he assured him.

Wilson nodded.

"I think if we're successful on this maiden voyage, we can take our pick of headquarters, Doc," Lee said as he watched the men at their various stations.

Wilson nodded.

"I'm going to walk the boat. See how everything is going." As Lee passed by the crewmembers at their stations, he glanced at the read-outs. The navigators were alert, and he nodded his approval.

"I'm joining you," Macon said. "Mr. Trent, you have the conn. Lay in a course to Kauai." He followed Lee the length of the command center and into the area once holding the missiles. A corridor ran down the middle of the space with science laboratories on either side. He knocked on one where he heard some noise.

"Come in," a feminine voice answered.

Lee opened the door and found Dr. Bailey Bennett in her white lab coat, smiling at him. She stood five feet five, petite, with long sun-bleached, light brown hair. Her blue eyes were her most striking feature.

"I just wanted to check the equipment. You know—nothing shifting around," she said.

Macon nodded. "Thank you, but we made sure everything would be safe during any voyage. On the surface or under. Dr. Wilson double-checked everything."

"Wonderful. Thank you so much. How far under the surface are we, Commander?"

"We are cruising a hundred feet under the surface and will maintain approximately that depth most of the way to

Hawaii," Macon said. "There will be a few drills and tests, but I will warn everyone of those."

"I am amazed at how smoothly something this big can run," she said. "Do you have a workout room?"

Lee nodded. "There is a small room aft of the science stations with a couple of treadmills, a bench with a few weights, and a rowing machine. Not a lot, but there are also some jogging courses mapped out in your introductory packet. Those are mainly places with enough room for you to run or jog,"

"Wonderful! Well, I guess I'll go to my cubby and get situated."

"Have a good evening, Ma'am," Mace said.

They continued on. Dr. Bennett disappeared down the stairs to the scientists' cabins.

They checked in with the reactor crew, then worked their way forward, visiting with the off-duty personnel, including the scientists.

"When are we going to begin our work?" Dr. Timothy Farr asked.

Lee remembered him as the zoologist whose assignment was checking on the monk seal population on Ni'ihau in Hawaii. "It will take us a little while to get to the islands, Doctor."

"I will take readings and samples as we travel, Captain Zuved."

"Sorry, I didn't know. After we are away from coastal traffic, you can begin your experiments," Lee told him. "Anytime you need to conduct experiments, make sure you add them to the scientific activities list."

"Yes, I'm sorry. I neglected to do that."

"No problem, Doctor. Just make sure anything requiring a change of speed or change of course be cleared with me,"

Mace reminded him, loud enough so the other scientists in the area could hear.

Lee had already advised them of this, but a reminder never hurt.

"Of course," Farr answered. "I gather samples with a slender arm extending several inches out from the port side of the sub in front of the propulsion jets."

They continued their tour of the boat. Everything from bow to stern worked well. "Mace, tomorrow, I would like for you to take her down several hundred feet and make sure everything continues to work as it should. Then return to our normal depth. Warn the crew before each of our maneuvers."

"Aye, Skipper." Mace grinned. "How does that sound, Lee?"

"Sounds satisfying." He felt awkward with the conversation. Mace went through the academy and sub school at the same time as he did. "This venture will work and you'll get your own boat."

"I don't doubt it, but I like the position I'm in right now. And you're right, this is the future."

He hadn't heard his friend talk with this much passion about research submarines during *Sea Dragon's* refitting. He nodded.

"So don't worry about me. I'm just glad we're on the same boat. In the normal navy, I doubt it would have ever happened."

Lee doubted it, too.

Chapter Ten

The scout ship came in directly over the south pole of the planet they chose. The supreme planner realized the error of such a steep descent as they passed into the outer layers of atmosphere. Then, the computers noticed something previously undetected. It caused the old engine distress. Then it caused more than distress.

Millin, what is wrong? Why is the ship shaking? asked one of the Leadership.

Several alarms blared. Some hadn't sounded for a millennium, from before the Great Wars. The wailing affronted the kreon, and it debilitated some of the old denbra.

Millin, the kreon planner, ordered his host to the main computer, ignoring the denbra's stiff fingers. With a moan, the host pushed the various buttons, bringing up statistics and showing views outside the ship.

Leader, there is something in the atmosphere interfering with the navigational computers!

Compensate or we'll crash! The supreme leader screamed in everyone's mind. He also sent his host to the main computer, despite the horrific gravitational forces gripping the ship. Another screaming alarm sounded with a denbra's terrified yelps. Smoke and sparks spit from several banks of machinery in the control room. Millin kept tight control over his host, despite the creature's pain. It moaned, groaned, and writhed as it stood at the main computer.

I think I can slow our descent, Leader, another kreon interjected in all the physical and telepathic noise.

Do it then!

The head navigator, a female kreon named Haliss, didn't answer. Her host dragged herself over to a different computer where stiff fingers beat a tattoo on the keyboard as fast as the kreon navigator could force it. Haliss encouraged her denbra to keep working. Her host cried out like the others but continued. Finally, the ship slowed, and the shuddering grew less violent. Several of the alarms slowed their jarring noise and then stopped altogether.

The monitors showed the ship making a more controlled descent toward the surface of the planet—toward a white, barren surface. They still traveled too fast.

Navigator, can you slow the ship more? We are descending too fast, Millin cried out.

I am trying, Leader. Haliss coaxed more from her host. The denbra continued pushing buttons her kreon directed her to push, although her legs shook with the effort of standing at the control panel. The ship slowed, even as it descended through the atmosphere. They shut blaring alarms off and watched the monitors show them a more controlled descent. Haliss realized they were still coming in too fast. *Flen, fire the front jets.*

The rockets slowed the ship a little. Then a little more. The ground rushed up. Rockets blasted until they ran out of fuel. The ship plowed into the ice and snow, skidded, and rolled once. It landed right side up and shuddered to a stop.

More alarms wailed, then the lights dimmed and emergency lights came on. The computers declared the ship intact, with damage the hosts could fix. The monitors showed the ship had plowed into enough snow and ice to hide them as well as cushion them from rocks and hard earth. Haliss's denbra groaned and collapsed to the deck. Hallis felt her heart falter, then it beat in a regular rhythm. The kreon felt sorry that her host had to experience these grueling hardships. The leader barked out orders. Now came the hard work.

Chapter Eleven

At the knock on his door, Lee closed the laptop containing the past day's statistics and performance reports. He glanced around his small cabin to make sure he'd put away his freshly cleaned laundry and picked up any trash. No problems there. "Enter."

Dr. Wendy Scherer, one of the marine biologists, entered. Her wet hair dripped on her tee shirt, uncombed. Her appearance suggested she had just gotten out of the shower. Usually buoyant and optimistic, Dr. Scherer's scowl told a different story.

"Captain Zuved. I have been very patient with the close quarters, trying to sleep with someone who snores, and someone who complains all the time. However, I don't think I can quite match my bodily functions with the need for the submarine to discharge its waste."

Doc Wilson had recruited Scherer early in his search and neither of them would want to lose her. Lee got up and pointed to his chair. "Please have a seat, Doctor, and let's see what we can work out." He slid out a folding chair stashed next to his small wardrobe and sat down.

With a huff, she plumped down in the chair. "I apologize for my appearance."

It always paid to listen to someone before making assumptions. "Your appearance is fine, Doctor. Um, did you have problems with the shower?" He hoped her complaint was that and not some other bathroom commodity.

"I would imagine you didn't get to this position without knowing most of what goes on." Scherer ran her fingers through her unruly hair.

"I also got this position by listening to people, especially if they are having problems."

"Even simple ones?" Dr. Scherer sighed.

"On a submarine, even simple ones aren't always simple." He leaned back to get comfortable on the tiny chair.

"I'll get used to living and working in the tight quarters. The showers are the size of coffins… And I'm still not sure I'm doing the commode right."

He smiled. "I have heard the racks, or rather, the beds, described as fancy coffins with curtains."

The doctor gave a short laugh. "I think my old high school locker had larger dimensions."

This time, Lee laughed. He pictured his high school locker. Three feet by one foot. Definitely an exaggeration, but he understood her dilemma.

She nodded. "It's all so strange."

Lee glanced around, taking in the narrow bunk, tiny chairs, the shared head, cubbies for his clothes and all his other belongings. But compared to anyone else's, it might as well be the Hilton. "Are you having problems with claustrophobia?"

She shook her head. "I don't feel closed in or anything like that. It's just things work differently. I feel like an imbecile when I don't remember the rules on how things, like commodes or showers, work on a submarine."

Lee took a deep breath. "Doctor..."

"Wendy, please."

"Only when we're not on duty. And I'm Lee."

She nodded.

"Why not put a reminder on a card and tape it to the wall next to the valve lever in the head where everyone can see it?"

Wendy blinked. "We can do that?"

He laughed softly. "Of course. There's not much space, but there's nothing sacred about the few inches available. And *Sea Dragon* isn't delicate, by any means."

She stood up. "Thank you, Lee." She ran her hand through her hair again. Then she grinned and began laughing. Wendy continued until the tears rolled down her cheeks.

Lee couldn't help it. He joined her, but not as hard and certainly not as long. Finally, he just waited until she stopped laughing.

"I never thought I'd be getting advice on how to use a bathroom."

"No problem," Lee replied with a chuckle. "I hope you'll ask if you have anything else you need help with." He remembered her other comment when she first came in. "Are you doing all right with your roommates?"

"Yes, I'm a somewhat light sleeper, especially in new circumstances. I have some earplugs to cut out the noise from them and the boat. To be honest, it's like sleeping in a hospital. Not a lot of privacy."

"Yes, definitely something to get used to. And by all means, use earplugs, even something to block out any light...."

"Red light," she groaned.

He immediately understood. "The red sleeping lights. To keep from waking up your roommates. You're right. It also takes some getting used to."

"How long did it take you?"

"About a week. I was a green and inexperienced ensign. Most of the time, I practically fell into my rack from exhaustion."

The scientist laughed. "Well, I appreciate your time."

"Please, ask me, Mister Macon, or Doc, if there's something confusing."

"I will. I guess if I want some breakfast, I'd better go finish cleaning up. And making a card to remind us." She laughed, and he joined her. "Oh, I might come and ask you how to play cribbage."

"I am not a great cribbage player, but if you ask Chief Bates, you'll learn all there is to the game."

"Which Chief Bates?"

"Either. Although I've heard Andrea Bates is a killer cribbage player. Of course, I wouldn't mind playing a game, so let me know when you want to."

"Tomorrow evening?"

He nodded. "I should be free for a while after the evening meal." As the door closed, he reminisced about his early submarine days. Lee folded up the extra chair, put it away, and opened his laptop.

Chapter Twelve

Lee sat across from Dr. Scherer at a table in the officer's wardroom. Someone had drilled cribbage board peg holes into the table and drawn the outline in magic marker. Someone else had embellished it with designs in the corners. Dr. Manuel Garcia sat next to his colleague, while Doc Wilson sat next to him.

Doc explained the basic rules while Lee shuffled the cards. He dealt five cards to each person.

Dr. Scherer took her cards, then looked up. "I'm a little concerned about Margie. She's really claustrophobic. I feel sorry for her except in the middle of the night when she wakes up screaming. Lord knows, I still feel sorry for her, but the rest of us are trying to sleep, too." She looked up, glancing around as though her roommate might be listening in. "Do you think you could talk to her? Discreetly, if you can. I, uh, don't want her to know I, sort of, tattled."

Lee sat back, pursed his lips, and lay down his cards. "So, she's trying to hide her problem?"

"I think she really wants to succeed, but I don't think she's winning the war against her fears."

"Do you know if she's talked to Ensign Meyers?" Lee asked. "There may be something he could do to help her."

Wendy shook her. "I'll mention it to her in the morning."

"Maybe I can talk with her, too," Doc added.

The game progressed slowly as the scientists took turns playing and learning. After three games, Lee yawned.

Doc laughed. "Go to bed."

He stood. "Aye, aye, boss." Turning to Dr. Scherer, he added, "I enjoyed the game."

She smiled and nodded.

Lee didn't waste time getting ready for bed and he fell asleep as soon as his head hit the pillow.

An insistent voice brought him out of his dreams. He jerked up to a dim light near his door and the annoying voice buzzing in his ear from the intercom. He answered. "Zuved here."

It was the officer of the watch. "Captain, there is an incident in forward quarters."

"I'll check on it." He slid out of bed and grabbed his trousers. Within a minute, he dashed out of his door. Macon met him. "You got a call, too?"

Mace nodded.

The scientists' quarters—specifically the women's quarters turned out to be the destination. Wendy Scherer met them and behind her, Lee heard screaming.

"She woke us up crying and when we tried to console her, she began screaming," Dr. Scherer explained. "She wouldn't let any of us sit next to her. Doctor Wilson went in and we heard a crash and… And we haven't heard from Rick lately. I worry she might have hurt him."

Lee stepped into the room lit with the red sleeping lights. He noticed someone sprawled on the floor, and someone else sitting nearby. Reaching behind him, he flipped on the regular light. Margie Prichard sat on the deck, holding Doc's head on her lap. He didn't move. Dr. Prichard screamed again and then she moaned, "I killed him! I killed him!"

Lee squatted down and tried talking in between Dr. Prichard's outcries. "Doctor Prichard. Margie." He studied Rick and saw his chest rising and falling. "Dr. Wilson is alive. You didn't kill him. Margie, do you hear me? He's not dead. Dr. Wilson isn't dead."

The screaming faltered. She glanced down. Her voice grew soft, but he heard her. "Not dead? But there's blood. He hit his head." She gave one more cry. Not as loud as before, but it echoed down the corridor.

"I can show you he's not dead."

A whispering voice behind him told the captain that Ensign Meyers had arrived.

He gave a hand signal to let the ensign know he heard him.

"Lee, I'll order *Sea Dragon* to the surface," Mace said before he slipped away.

Grateful for Mace's quick response, Lee returned his attention to the distressed scientist. "Margie, let me show you Dr. Wilson is okay." He crawled forward but stopped when she tensed. "What happened, Margie?"

She whimpered and moaned again. "I don't know. I thought something horrible came to get me. Some kind of monster. The next thing I knew, I heard a groan, and I saw Rick laying on the floor, blood everywhere." She moaned again.

"Let's check him together." He slid another few inches, heartened when she ignored his advance. He touched Doc's foot, then his ankle. "Doc Wilson's alive."

"You sure he's not dead?"

Lee felt the sub rise, a subtle sensation most non-submariners didn't discern right away, but Margie evidently did.

"What's happening? Something's happening."

"Yes. *Sea Dragon's* rising to the surface. I thought you might like to see the stars."

"What? Stars? But what about Doctor Wilson?"

"We were going to check him together." Lee had reached Dr. Prichard but didn't touch her yet. He felt for a pulse in Doc's leg. The heartbeat sounded strong. "Feel for Dr. Wilson's pulse on his neck."

She stared at him, her eyes unfocused.

Lee scooted forward and gently put his hand on hers. She shivered, blinked at him, and then zoned out. Her eyes closed, and she sagged sideways. Lee held her close to his body while Eric Meyers kneeled on the deck next to Doc. He checked the scientist's pulse and blood pressure before he inched closer and injected Margie with a sedative. Her whole body relaxed as she fell into unconsciousness.

"Where do you want me to take her, Eric?"

"My office. I can keep a better watch on her there."

Lee nodded and got to his feet, her limp body held tightly in his arms. Wendy gazed at her roommate's face and asked, "May I accompany you, Captain?"

"Of course. I don't think she'll wake up. Still, it certainly would help for you to be there if she did." Lee carried Margie through the narrow corridor, to the miniscule sick bay on the same level. His arm muscles were burning by the time he reached Eric's office. Eric had pulled down the rack and Lee slid her onto it. He backed off to let the CMO work.

Lee stayed out in the corridor when two of the crew brought in Doc. Eric pointed to the other pull-down rack for

Wilson. He ignored Margie for the moment. As the CMO took vitals and cleaned up *Sea Dragon's* boss, Lee waited. Wendy stayed in the corridor with him.

"How is he?" he finally asked, peering into the cubby.

"Doc has a nice lump on the back of his head and a small gash," Eric said as he worked. "I'm going to stitch it up while he's out. Vitals are pretty good. I think Dr. Prichard had an anxiety attack, pushed Dr. Wilson away from her. He hit his head on the edge of a rack and down he went. Don't think there is a concussion, but I'm going to treat him like there is. I'll know more when I wake him up."

"Let me know when he's coherent, Eric. You need us anymore?"

Meyers shook his head. "No, sir. I'm going to keep Dr. Prichard sedated for the next day or so. Then she won't become too anxious. You did a good job, Captain."

"Thanks." Lee motioned to Dr. Scherer, and they walked down the corridor back to her cabin. "I am going to have to have Dr. Prichard transferred off ship when we get to Hawaii."

Wendy nodded. "She's a very talented oceanographer, and she wanted so much to be a part of this. I'm sorry this happened."

"Did Dr. Prichard have any inkling she would have trouble onboard?"

"No, she didn't. I think she joked about an MRI test one time."

"Those are worse than a submarine," Lee said. "At least the early ones were." They reached the women's cabin. Someone had already cleaned up the mess. "Will you be all right? I think we have other places where you two can sleep if you'd like."

"No, Captain. I think my roommate is already asleep and I'll be fine. By the way, have you had to deal with what happened to Margie a lot?"

Lee shook his head. "Actually, in all my naval career, this is only the second time I have dealt with a case of claustrophobia. Most Navy men have enough training to figure out if they are incompatible for submarine service before they receive their assignments. And submarine duty is a voluntary job. I can guess you folks get very little training."

She smiled. "We got a pep talk from Rick, a grand tour and a very large safety manual."

"That's not much help."

"At least we're not too far from Honolulu if anyone else has issues," Wendy said.

"Just call the officer of the watch in the control room if you need a change of sleeping quarters."

"You have been very kind to all of us. Thank you."

He nodded and left for the control room. They'd be able to return to their course and depth. Lee gave the orders and then returned to his cabin. It took him a while to get back to sleep. He realized they had been remiss in not better preparing the scientists for this kind of experience. When Doc recovered, he'd have to discuss this with him.

Chapter Thirteen

Wilson stood next to Lee as the submarine slowly approached the dock near the Kauai Naval testing area. The breeze felt warm and refreshing. The trip had taken just over four and a half days, and other than Margie's anxiety attack, went smoothly. Lee and Mace had insisted on various drills, so the scientists were as familiar with any emergency as the crew.

The *Dragon* eased in smoothly. The shore crew threw tethers to the waiting men on the deck, and they soon tied *Sea Dragon* off.

Ensign Meyers and Macon helped Dr. Prichard off the boat and to a waiting ambulance. Within an hour half the complement of the *Sea Dragon* was disgorging to explore the island.

"Which scientists do you have running their experiments during the first watch?" Lee asked Doc. They had observed the group of shore leavers heading off the boat in a variety of garb from the garish beach shirts to halfway suited up. A few had on jeans and tee shirts.

"Farr is heading over to Ni'ihau within the hour to study the seals. Milly, Rennie, Mark, and I are going to dive out to the corals and take samples. A few of my colleagues are setting up the labs to receive the samples."

"Who's going with Farr?"

"He said he didn't need anyone to accompany him."

"I think he needs a partner."

"I think he had a bit of claustrophobia on the trip and is self-conscious about it."

"So, you're letting him go alone?"

"I told him to take a crewmember with scientific as well as diving experience, but I suspect he said yes to get me off his back."

"Submarine rules. I'll have a talk with him."

"Good luck, Lee."

"No luck about it. He needs to follow the rules or find a laboratory on the mainland to work in."

Doc nodded.

Lee climbed back in the boat and headed toward the science section. He found Farr coming out of his cabin, some of his gear in hand. The scientist appeared ready to count seals. "Who's going out with you, Doctor?"

Farr stared at him for a moment. "I'm going to get a couple of Ni'ihauen natives to help me."

"Nothing wrong with that, but the first rule of *Sea Dragon* is we do nothing without a partner."

"I…. Well, I…."

Lee lowered his voice. "Used to working alone, I gather."

Farr started, then nodded.

"And I understand, but you're working on a submarine and we have to count on one another. No matter what our jobs are."

Farr opened his mouth, but nothing came out.

"Getting used to working on a boat traveling underwater is difficult, too." He paused. "I might have a solution if you're okay with it."

"Oh?"

"I'll accompany you."

"You?"

Lee grinned. "My other degree is marine biology. I enjoyed it very much. Been a long time."

"Are you serious?"

"Absolutely. It's one reason I left the more stable position I had and took on this job. Let me change into something a little better suited for climbing on rocks and through sand, and I'll meet you on the pier. Take me only a moment."

"Better shoes, too," Farr ventured.

"Of course," he said, looking down at his no-slip boat shoes most submariners wore on board. "I'll have a crewmen break out our motor launch. Do you think you'll want to do some diving as well?"

"I'm not sure what we'll find with the census on the beach," Farr said. "The owner of the island contacted me to check if the population is declining again. Why don't we check out the situation and then bring diving gear tomorrow if we feel the need?"

"Sounds like a plan. We don't have more than a half a day today, anyway."

Lee returned to his cabin, dug into his closet, and quickly changed. Someone knocked as he finished.

"It's me," Macon called out before he could say anything.

"Enter."

Mace came in and took in the activity in a glance. "So, you're going ashore. Great!"

"I am accompanying Dr. Farr to Ni'ihau."

"How did you manage that? He makes a clam sound like a chatterbox."

Lee shrugged as he pulled out sturdier walking shoes. "I just made him aware of our rule and told him I had a science degree, too."

"What rule?"

"The rule saying we don't go out alone."

"Isn't it mainly for underwater excursions?"

"I think it should apply to any excursion other than sight-seeing. And even then, we've been in some hairy ports of call."

Mace laughed. "Well, have fun counting seals."

"I plan on it! And you?"

"I'll watch the boat until you get back."

Lee smiled. "Trent can take a watch."

"I know, but I'd like to do the first watch, especially since you're taking off at the last minute."

"Got to build relationships."

Macon nodded, and Lee left his little room, whistling.

Chapter Fourteen

The temperate breeze brought smells of flowers, while the small waves rocked the boat. The seventeen mile ride seemed over with too quickly. Patterson guided them to Ni'ihau while Lee sat across from Farr and watched the distant shore draw closer. Sea birds dipped to check them out, then wheeled back up in the sky. There were several varieties, but he didn't recognize their names.

"Koa e' ula," Farr said, almost absently.

"A what?"

"A koa e'ula. The Hawaiian name for a Red-tailed Tropicbird. They nest near here. We may see their colonies as we do our seal watch."

"They are graceful. Are they endangered?"

"Not the last I heard."

In the distance, a large shape rose out of the water and then fell back down. A whale, humpback. Lee pointed, and Farr nodded.

Soon they were pulling into a smallish jetty and boat dock on Ni'ihau. Patterson jumped out with a rope and tied the small boat to the pier. Lee and Farr climbed out with the cameras and recording equipment. A middle-aged Hawaiian came out to greet them, dressed only in shorts.

"Aloha! Welcome!" he boomed. "You are from *Sea Dragon*?"

"Yes, sir. I'm Captain Lee Zuved and this is Dr. Timothy Farr."

The man shook both their hands and Lee felt all of his fingers trying to meld together.

When he could politely pull away, he checked his fingers. He heard Farr sucking in his breath.

"I will have to sail over and see this big accomplishment of yours," the man said. "My name is Iosepa Kahale."

"Mr. Kahale…." Farr began.

"Iosepa, please."

"Iosepa, then. We are here to check on your monk seals."

Iosepa shook his head. "There are fewer than last year."

"Have you counted them?"

"I don't need to count. I can tell. Fewer pups, fewer mothers. Not as many seals this year. There seem to be fewer and fewer."

"Do you have the count for last year?"

"Yes, up in the boathouse. I will go get it. Wait here."

Iosepa strode up the small hill.

"Do you know where the seal nursery is?" Lee asked.

"Yes, not too far west."

"Let's start up the hill and meet him halfway."

By now, Patterson had joined them and relieved them of some of the recording equipment.

"I believe that's a good plan. There's no telling how long it will take him to find last year's paperwork."

Just as the words finished coming from Farr's mouth, the Hawaiian came back out and hurried down the hill. "Here!" he called out, waving the paper. He handed it to Farr, who studied it for a moment before handing it to Lee.

"About nine hundred individuals, including the new pups."

"Yes. We had about a thousand the year before. There are fewer this year."

"You keep this for the moment," Farr handed back the document. "We'll probably want the figures later when we do this count."

"Very good. Do you know the way?"

"I believe so. I studied the map."

"Follow this path and you will come on the nurseries soon enough. Be careful. The pups are still very young and some females are very protective. I'll come up there a little later."

"Thanks," Lee called as they headed up the path to the seal's beach.

When they crossed over a hill to the beach, they stopped in shock. The beach only contained sand. No seals, no pups.

"Where are the seals, sir?" Patterson asked.

"That's a good question," Lee returned. He didn't hear any seals in the distance. Only the seabirds and the waves slapping against the rocks. "It's April. There should be all kinds of seals and pups."

The scene rendered Farr speechless.

"What would cause them all to disappear? There is nothing scientific about this!"

Lee walked down close to the waterline, seeing nothing. No blood, no evidence of violence. Environmentalists had designated this as a seal nursery. No one could do anything to disturb the animals. Watchers had spotted seals here as recently as two days ago. Lee gazed across the water, looking for some clues. He saw nothing. Then he spied a dark speck on the horizon—manmade, not a whale. Lee dashed back to the equipment and grabbed the camera with the longest telephoto lens.

"What?" Farr asked as he picked up the other camera.

"Something out on the water," he called over his shoulder.

It took a minute to get the telephoto settings coordinated to his best advantage. The top of a large yacht came into focus. From the spray, it appeared to be a hydrofoil. With the reefs exposed and just below the surface, it didn't seem too wise. "Seems too close to land where those kinds of ships aren't wanted," he mumbled.

Farr stood next to him. "What do you think it could be?"

"Not sure."

"What is going on?" Iosepa hollered from the top of the hill.

"Come on down here," Lee called back. "See if you recognize this."

For all his size, the Hawaiian fairly flew down the hill and over the rocky dune. He peered out over the ocean.

"Here, look through this," Lee said, handing the man his camera.

Lee waited as Iosepa gazed through the camera lens.

"What business does a boat like that have here?" the Hawaiian muttered.

"I wondered the same thing." Still, Lee thought, except for the 'take-off' of a hydrofoil, they were quieter than a freighter or passenger ship.

"Could they have taken the seals?" Iosepa asked.

"Seems far-fetched to me," Lee began. "How in the world would they get them on the ship?"

Iosepa shook his head. "I need to let the authorities know about this."

"Do you have a motorboat or motor launch?"

The Hawaiian gazed at him for a couple of seconds and then nodded. "Follow me." Iosepa ran as fast back up the hill as he had come down.

Lee slung the camera over his shoulder and dashed after Iosepa. Farr slipped through the sand right behind him. Something about all this gave Lee a bad feeling. "Gather up the rest of the equipment, Pat. We're going for a ride."

"Yes, sir!"

It still didn't take him long to get back to the jetty. He gazed at Iosepa's motorboat and grimaced, wondering if it would fall apart if he took it faster than rowboat speed. Their launch wouldn't match what he had seen out on the water, but at least it wouldn't fall apart and its size might keep them from being seen.

"Pat, let's take our boat." Lee could hear Patterson sigh.

"I'd like to come, too," Farr said.

"Get in, then."

Patterson untied the skiff and jumped in. This time, Lee took the controls, and they were off before anyone on shore realized what they were doing.

"Get the walkie out and contact the XO. Let him know we are following a suspicious boat maybe having something to do with the disappearance of a colony of seals. Have him contact the Coast Guard."

"Aye, aye, sir."

He almost flew around the reef, bouncing off the tops of the waves. "Can you see anything, Doctor?"

Farr had a pair of binoculars, searching. "Not seeing anything yet."

Enough time had elapsed for the hydrofoil to have gone in any direction. There were so many atolls and small islands. Then again, where would twenty-five seals be hiding?

"Wait a minute. I think I see something—barely."

"Which direction?"

Farr pointed.

Without saying a word, Lee revved the motor again, maneuvered the rudder and they were flying off after the boat.

"It's getting harder to see. They have to be going incredibly fast."

"Those kinds of boats can go incredibly fast."

"What are we trying to accomplish?"

"If we can keep them in sight until we can figure out where they're going, then when the Coast Guard shows up, they have the big guns, and might find these guys."

"I can't see them anymore." Farr's voice held deep disappointment.

"I think I know their direction, sir," Patterson said. The sailor pulled out a small notebook, gazed at the last direction they had seen the mysterious ship, and the position of the sun. "Not very accurate, but hopefully better than nothing."

"This would be a good time to have those trained dolphins on board," Lee muttered. "Nothing would leave them behind."

"Trained dolphins, sir?"

"It's one of Dr. Wilson's future dreams, Pat," he responded. "Someday he'd like to work with dolphins or whales."

Chapter Fifteen

"Captain Zuved, we can't go on unsubstantiated hunches," the Coast Guard lieutenant explained.

To Lee's ear, the young officer sounded a bit patronizing. They were on the deck of the Coast Guard cutter, trying to explain what had happened. "Aren't you also trying to save these seals?" He peered at the nametag. "Lt. Owens."

"Of course, sir!"

"Then it wouldn't hurt to find this ship and ask them a few questions."

Owens rubbed his chin. "We'll go out and see if there is anything out there."

"Thanks, Lieutenant. We're returning to *Sea Dragon*. When you're finished, the head of our mission, Dr. Rick Wilson, would be interested in hearing the results of your search."

Owens nodded, and Lee climbed down into the skiff. Patterson revved up the motor. By the time they reached the *Dragon*, the sun had set.

***

"How in the hell could a couple dozen seals disappear?" Doc asked at the dinner table.

Lee shook his head. "I don't have a clue, but our assignment here seems to have increased in importance. Especially since the Coast Guard didn't find any sign of the hydrofoil."

Doc stared into his coffee cup. "Damn, that's frustrating."

"Are there any unaffected seal populations?" Lee asked.

Doc glanced up. "Several. We can head out to Midway and check one of those rookeries."

Lee nodded his agreement. "I'll go over the logistics with Mace. We might have to place divers at the various seal rookeries to keep watch."

Doc frowned. "Wouldn't that be dangerous?"

Lee shook his head. "If we were trying to arrest these people, it might. But we need to find out who these poachers are. So, we stay hidden with cameras. Whether it ends up being the mysterious boat or someone else, we have to find out what's going on."

"I agree." Doc finished his now cold coffee.

"We need to get this set up tonight. These people, whoever they are, need to be caught in the act. Once the season is over, we won't have a snowball's chance in hell."

"You're right. I leave the logistics up to you, Lee, but I will be part of this."

"You need to coordinate everything. From the *Dragon*."

Doc growled his displeasure.

"You'll know what's going on everywhere in real time," Lee reasoned.

"Who do you suggest should go out?"

"Those with advanced diving and maybe a little Seal training," he answered.

"I thought you said there'd be no interaction." Doc frowned. "I don't want anyone hurt."

"I did, Doc, but we also need to have people who can defend themselves," explained Lee.

Doc nodded. "Okay. How many do we have that fit in both categories?"

Lee did some quick math. "About six."

Doc Wilson slid out of his chair. "Let's go plot this out."

The skipper followed him. They made a bee-line toward the control room, directly above them.

Macon stood watch with the officer of the deck, Mark Ellis. "Got some orders?"

"Yes. We're going to do surveillance and try to figure out who these characters are."

"Drones or personal surveillance?" Macon asked.

"Personal, mostly, although sending out some drones would be a good idea, too. We'll use all the skiffs and stake out the islands with seal populations."

"Who do you propose?"

"All expert divers who have some Seal training. The idea someone could jerk a bunch of seals off a beach under our noses irritates the hell outa me. It's a personal affront."

"All right, Lee. Let's figure this out. The distances between these atolls and islands are quite far." Macon typed instructions into a computer and studied the map on the monitor.

"I know." Lee studied the map.

"Captain? Incoming message for you," the intercom announced.

Walking the short distance to the communications station, Lee asked, "What's up, Mark?"

"You wanted a status report on the seals, sir?"

Lee nodded.

"Wildlife Management says the Regway Atoll is empty of seals. There were eight adults there yesterday."

Lee muttered under his breath. "Tell them thanks."

"They want to know if you are planning to investigate, sir."

"Tell them we certainly are investigating. We'll head out there tonight."

"Aye, aye."

Twenty-four hours later, an hour after sunset, Lee and Petty Officer Hall pulled their small inflatable skiff into the shadows of an outcropping of scrubby, windblown trees. The winds were warm, and the pair pulled out their equipment in silence. They hid everything, including the skiff, under brush and behind trees.

Lee heard seal noises beyond the brush, giving him a reason to smile. Only a small group of seals used this tiny atoll, so scientists made observations from boats offshore. He motioned to his partner, and they crept up the small rise toward the seals. When the pinnipeds were in sight, Lee hunkered down behind some rocks and pulled out his night vision binoculars.

At first, nothing seemed out of the ordinary. The females laid with their pups, some of whom suckled contentedly. After an hour, when both men yawned in boredom, the adults heaved up and pulled themselves toward the shore, barking and waving their heads back and forth. Lee knew seals did this occasionally, but it didn't seem like normal behavior. The younger seals waited but whined their displeasure. Lee estimated the pups to be about half the age they would be when their mothers left them.

The strange behavior continued, with the mothers edging closer to the waves. Finally, one pulled herself into the surf, then another, and another.

"Getting any readings of other vessels?" Lee whispered.

Hall checked his instruments. "Yes, sir. Straight out, quarter mile. Should we get the skiff?"

"We need to see what happens here first." Lee still had his binoculars trained on the seals. He had already activated the camera feature, so Doc could see everything in real time on the *Dragon*.

Like a cork out of a bottle, all the adult seals dove into the water. The pups pulled themselves closer to the waves. They made soft sounds—whimpering. Their dark heads wove back and forth. A few entered the water, a little more slowly than their mothers. Lee could see their heads bobbing and flippers splashing, but finally the only thing he could hear were waves breaking against the rocks. *What in the world have we just witnessed?* The other pups backed away, still whimpering.

"Now, we get the skiff," he hissed. They raced as fast as they could back along the path, grabbing their diving equipment and loading it on the boat. Pushing off, they leaped in and Lee started the engine.

"Sir?"

"I'm assuming they are only interested in the seals. Or they already know we are here and can't keep up with them. Whatever it is, I want to see if there is anything else we can find out tonight."

"Why don't I steer and you work the instruments, sir?"

Lee left the steering to his partner and consulted his comp-pad. As it had for Hall, it showed a vessel about a half mile out from the atoll and slowly moving farther. "Slow us down. Half speed. They aren't in a hurry. Probably because of the seals. Don't want to run into them."

Hall said nothing as he followed the orders.

Lee pulled on his diving gear. If Hall had questions, he didn't ask them. "Stop the motor," ordered. He checked the tanks, pulled on his helmet, and activated the night lens. Then he handed the computer pad to Hall and fell backward into the water. The night lens made the reef brighter, but not like daylight. Shadows were menacing and Lee felt the goosebumps rising on his arms.

He swam toward the craft, not hearing the revving of the hydrofoil's engines. Without better light, Lee couldn't be sure, but something told him this was the same boat he had seen earlier. He swam about thirty feet under the water.

Something came into shadowy view. A large herd of seals swam behind the boat. A variety of indistinct noises surrounded him. *What's enticing them? Why would they leave their pups?* Lee swam among them, using the animals as camouflage. Occasionally, one would bump against him, but they avoided touching him. Right now, they were shielding him from observation by anyone on the boat.

All the seals passed him. He continued swimming, keeping his flashlight off. His night vision lens showed a very large shape ahead, and he slowed down.

After several minutes, an engine started with a muffled roar. They were leaving. What did they want with the seals? Lee took a chance and slowly surfaced. All the seals had disappeared.

The hydrofoil rocked gently about fifty feet ahead of him. Lee pulled the small camera from his front pocket and took several pictures. Then he opened the camera lens all the way to show more detail. As the boat roared away, he stuck the camera back into the zippered pocket. The hydrofoil engaged almost immediately, and the stacked-up waves and wind shoved him back.

Lee swam back to the skiff. He wanted to see the condition of the remaining seal pups. Hall assisted him aboard and then helped him slip off his tank. They came to a seal pup bobbing on the surface. The two men snagged a flipper and dragged it on board. It coughed and struggled to get out of Lee's grasp, but he held on to it. Nearby, a shark darted out to the open ocean, with a seal pup in its jaws. Hall increased his speed, and they soon arrived back on the shore. Lee climbed out with the pup in a tight grip. He let it go on dry land and watched the young pinniped struggle over the loose sand to the other young seals.

The pups called for their mothers. Why had these guys stayed on shore while the others, including the ones on Ni'ihau, had leaped into the water after the adults? Lee hoped their cameras held enough information to catch these poachers.

The seals backed away from him as he pulled out his flashlight and counted them.

Soft huffing told him Hall approached. The pups backed even further away. "I called the *Dragon,* sir, and told them the status of our watch. *Sea Dragon's* ten miles north of our position, waiting for everyone else's reports. Did you want to head back?"

"No, we have an island with eight hungry seal pups. We can't leave them. Let me have the communicator." Hall handed him the long-range radio.

"Sparks?" The skipper waited a moment. "Get Dr. Wilson." He waited a few more seconds, his thoughts not the least bit soothed by the gentle waves and soft breeze. "Doc? Lee. I'll tell you more later, but we have eight pups several weeks too young to venture out in the water. Their mothers took off without them and I'm not leaving them here alone."

"I'll let the wildlife management know your status. Will you two be all right on the atoll till morning?" Doc asked.

"Don't know why not. I'm going to see if I can find something they can eat."

"They're probably too young for solid food."

"It's worth a try. Maybe a soft lobster?" Lee replied.

"We'll swing around tomorrow after we pick up everyone else."

"All right. Zuved out." Lee pulled his tanks back on. "Watch the pups, Hall. Don't let them in the water. I'm going hunting."

"Yes, sir."

Lee nodded and finished putting his gear on. He took a spear gun this time and turned on his lamp, then he walked into the surf and pulled on his flippers.

Chapter Sixteen

Normally, Lee loved night diving. He switched on the soft light in his helmet. This allowed him to see any dangers, but not overwhelm the creatures. The fan corals waved languidly. Several enormous fish swam by as though they had no cares in the world. A moray eel darted partway out of its hole and then squeezed back in. Lee swam further out, just where the shelf dropped into darkness. Something round and out of place hovered just above the ocean floor. Lee swam closer and let his light shine full on it. Several small crustaceans were picking at the seal pup.

He frowned but could do nothing about it. As he hunted, Lee spied a few more carcasses. The Hawaiian Monk seal could ill afford this kind of attrition. He wondered who could do such a thing. The skipper put one of the dead pups in his specimen bag. Lee struggled to get the heavy animal into the net bag, but he knew Doc would want to examine it. About halfway through his tank of air, Lee found one of the local lobsters and caught it. It went into his quarry bag. He made his way back to the beach, where the rest of the seals still called for their mothers.

A couple of them tried to push toward him, but Lee waved his arms and they backed off.

"Did you find something they might like, sir?" Hall asked.

"A lobster. We'll break it up and try to make the meat as soft as we can."

They worked on getting the seals to accept some of the meat with limited success. The older pups ate small pieces, but they did so as they continued crying. Lee laid the specimen sack on a rock.

"What did you find, sir?"

"A pup trying to follow its mother. There were several on the ocean floor. Figured Doc would want one to examine."

"Damn!"

"Yeah," Lee replied. "Why don't you try to get a bit of shut-eye and I'll watch the pups?"

"Wake me after a bit, sir."

"I will." Soon, he heard soft snoring. Young sailors seemed to have a knack for falling asleep quickly and in the strangest places. He gazed out toward the surf. A brightening on the horizon told him the moon would rise soon. A bird behind him screeched and made him jump. The seal pups were laying on the sand, sleeping as soundly as Seaman Hall.

The moon rose over the horizon. Its light shone brightly and he could see everything on the beach. One pup pulled itself over to nuzzle Lee's back.

"Sorry, my friend, I can't give you that kind of meal." He still had a piece of the lobster the seals hadn't eaten. Holding it out to the inquisitive creature, Lee tried to coax the pinniped to eat. It nibbled the piece of meat and swallowed it. Then it lay down next to him with a moan.

Lee waited until the moon shone almost directly above him before he woke Hall. Then he tried to emulate his partner.

The skipper dozed but didn't think he slept until he felt a nuzzle under his armpit. Opening his eyes, he saw the sun half over the horizon. Lee gazed at the seal but didn't try touching it. It wouldn't do to have them get too accustomed to humans. Of course, the pups were going to have to go to a wildlife rehab center.

The other pups began making demands for food.

"Sorry, kids. I wish I could accommodate you."

"Skipper, there's a boat approaching."

Lee pulled out his binoculars and studied their visitor. A forty-foot catamaran from the local wildlife center approached their position. He stood and waved. It didn't take long for the boat to run up on the sand enough for two of the four men on board to jump down and greet him.

"Captain Zuved?" the first one asked.

He nodded. "And you?"

The man held out his hand. Lee shook it.

"Dr. William Dolan, head zoologist at the Pinniped Marine Center." He studied the pups, who swayed back and forth and making plaintive calls. "The mothers just headed out to sea?"

"Without even a backward glance," Lee replied. "Several of the pups tried to follow, but either sharks were waiting, or the seals just weren't developed enough to swim out in the open ocean."

"Hell's bells!" Dolan pointed to his partner. "Doctor Hank Pilson, marine behaviorist. He's been out here on the islands trying to figure out just what's going on."

Lee and Pilson also shook hands. "Can I assume you might need our help loading these youngsters up?"

"We'd appreciate it, Captain. We have a cage big enough to hold them and a winch capable of raising it, but herding eight pups into a strange enclosure won't appeal to them."

The men on the ship lowered the cage to the sand and Pilson opened the door as far as it would go. Lee and Hall tried herding the seals toward the enclosure. The pups weren't buying it. They backed off or scattered.

"I think we're going to have to lasso them and pull them in," Pilson said.

"Let me try this one," Lee suggested. He dug out a piece of lobster from one claw and held it out for the seal who had been chummy. It came closer—then closer, sniffing hungrily. He tossed the meat into the cage and the seal pup checked it out. It didn't like the feel of the metal floor but stayed inside. Lee, Hall, and three others pushed seals into the enclosure while the sixth person tried to keep the pups from backing out.

"Just like herding cats!" Hall grumbled.

Lee laughed. "Cats are easier."

Dolan latched the door. The men were rewarded with a coating of sweat and sand, and a couple of nips from the recalcitrant pups. The winch carefully pulled the cage onto the deck of the ship, with accompanying barking protests.

"By the way, do you want a ride back to your fancy submarine?" Dolan asked.

"Let me contact *Sea Dragon* and see where they are."

"We have you in sight," Doc told him on the radio. "Have them bring you out here."

"Okay, Doc." He passed along the word.

***

It didn't take long for Lee to clean up and don a fresh uniform. Doc studied the pictures taken the day before. Peering over his shoulder, the captain saw an enlarged picture of the hovercraft.

"You make this out?" Doc asked him. He handed the skipper his magnifying glass.

"Looks like some kind of logo," He replied. "But I can't figure out what it's for. I think Petty Officer Tyler could figure this out. He's good with technology and knows how to make it work for you."

"Thanks, Lee." Doc scratched behind his ear. "I know I have seen something similar, but I can't place it to save me."

"Let me call Tyler and have him report to you."

As Lee predicted, it didn't take Tyler long to figure out the boat's origin. It belonged to a billionaire living on a privately owned island eight hundred miles south of the Hawaiian archipelago. Doc and Tyler did the research, and then called Lee, the XO, and the Chief of the Boat, Terrill Bates, to a meeting.

Tyler spoke first. "Captain, first I found out who the logo belonged to. Then I figured out the hydrofoil's destination. The island of Kalura is privately owned by several high rollers, er, I mean billionaires. They've built a huge hotel called South Winds Luxury Pacific Entertainment Center, and it rivals Disneyland. It's the destination of many jet-setting billionaires."

"I don't know why someone with so much money and prestige would want to poach seals," Doc said, pacing the length of the wardroom.

"Seal skin coats?" Bates ventured.

"Any guess could be the right answer, Chief. However, while this guy has at least part ownership of the opulent hotel, he and his partners are very private. The public only sees what the owners want them to see," Doc replied.

"Who is this guy?" Macon asked.

Tyler answered. "Roger Rollings. I don't have names for any of his partners yet, but I'm close."

The XO whistled. "I've heard of him. He had a wildlife sanctuary on the mainland until the government shut it down because of shady practices. The prevailing rumor said the tigers were being farmed. No one ever got the low-down on him. It happened a decade ago, and he's been clean, at least on the surface, making money hand over fist out here ever since. Of course, he's living on a privately owned island where the United States government doesn't have any jurisdiction."

"Perhaps he's doing wildlife stuff, but just not doing it publicly," Bates suggested.

"Then we have to find out why he's apparently taking critically endangered seals," Lee replied. "I don't think we can wait for the wheels of government to study and decide the problem. Not with the extinction of a species at risk." Here, he thought, it would be easier to beg forgiveness rather than try to get permission.

"But how?" Doc asked. He continued pacing.

Lee shrugged. "A few of us have had a little experience with subterfuge. We coordinate with the wildlife organization out here, as well as the local Office of Naval Intelligence office at Pearl. I think they'll help us because they don't want the extinction of a native mammal to occur on their watch if there's a way to prevent it." He smiled. "And besides, the government might be very interested in taking down someone who has screwed them out of due process."

Doc nodded. "We'd better hustle before we lose more seals."

Chapter Seventeen

Lee re-read the personnel records in front of him, absently taking a sip from his so-so lukewarm coffee. Doc pushed a fresh cup across the table. "You are a mind reader. Thanks."

A soft knock and Petty Officer Maria Sanchez stepped into Science Lab One. Lee hadn't told her why he requested her to the meeting. Her eyes showed curiosity and a little anxiety. He understood the feeling well, having been called to a few offices in his younger years.

She stood stiffly in front of the table. "Reporting as requested, Captain."

Lee smiled. "This is informal, Sanchez. Have a seat and I'll explain what I need." He glanced at the door, hoping the Bates's were right behind her. Since they weren't, he would let Sanchez know the plan. Let her get over the shock.

"Yes, sir." She sat down, the curiosity still highlighting her eyes.

"You took some intelligence classes. Training for ONI?"

"I thought I wanted to go into ONI after I enlisted." She paused, glancing at both men before continuing. "I guess a lot of new recruits thought the same thing."

Lee nodded. "Cryptology, languages. A very popular career in the Navy."

"I have a talent with languages, so I took the classes. By the time submarine service opened up for women, I changed over, but it's still come in handy."

"The reason I'm asking," Lee began. "We're working with several agencies, including ONI, trying to find out who's poaching the Hawaiian monk seals and why. Four of us are going to find out by pretending to be filthy rich visitors to a famous resort. We need someone to pose as my wife."

Her mouth dropped open. "Me?" she squeaked.

He nodded, "Yes. I hope that doesn't bother you." She shook her head, but her eyes were still wide, like a deer in the headlights. "The most likely suspect is Roger Rollings. I photographed one of his ships near an island where about a half dozen seals disappeared. Chief Bates and his wife will join us as well." He paused. "There could be some danger."

"If it helps save an endangered species, then I'll gladly help, sir."

"Thanks," Doc said.

Someone else tapped on the door and Doc motioned for Terrill and Andrea Bates to join them.

"Sorry, sir. Finishing an inspection…."

"Don't worry about it, Chief. This is informal. You two are going to accompany Sanchez and me to South Winds Luxury Pacific Entertainment Center. We're going to find out the connection with the disappearing seals."

Bates whistled. "Wow! How are we going to infiltrate something like that, sir? We going in as bus boys or cooks?"

Lee laughed. "Neither. We go in as high rollers. And before anyone protests, it's being bankrolled by the government. We're going to be guests and act as though we are among the high and mighty."

"I've never been high and mighty, sir," Andrea Bates said.

Sanchez giggled softly before cutting it off.

"Neither have I," he replied, "but we are the four who have the best background for this."

"What background, Skipper?" Bates asked. "I don't have any spy training."

"Didn't you tell me a few months ago you and your wife met at a community theater gig in your hometown?"

"Oh."

"My understanding is you're still periodically doing some performances. Didn't you two play parts in a stage version of *The Color Purple* in Bremerton?"

"Yes, sir."

"You are going in pretending to be something you're not."

"We don't have to pretend everything, sir. Do we?" Bates pulled his wife closer.

Doc shook his head, then laughed. "Don't enjoy yourselves too much." He opened up his computer and booted it up. "Look at what you're going to be digging around in."

The next half hour, the group perusing pictures of the resort, including the aquatic show, the beaches, and the various parts of the hotel.

Sanchez asked, "How are we going to find evidence of poaching? This place appears to be on the up and up."

"Good question," Lee said. "I will do a bit of reconnoitering, but we're all going out at night. The folks in charge of this agree we don't need to be there longer than a night, possibly two. They believe we'll find what we need somewhere near the aquatic area." He motioned for Doc to pull up a diagram and maps of the resort. resort buildings and entertainment areas covered most of the island, leaving enough beach to satisfy the needs of the vacationers. "We have a great deal of detailed information about everything except the aquatic area. That's where we will concentrate most of our efforts."

Bates began laughing. "Can't help but think the guys footing the bill for this don't want us taking our time spying. Too expensive."

"I didn't ask, Chief, but I wouldn't doubt it."

Doc closed his laptop and cleared his throat. "I don't have a clue what would entice someone to poach already critically endangered creatures, but we have to take some action. Even what we're doing here might be too late."

"But we're going to try." Lee remembered the baby seals orphaned back on the rocky island. "We'll get the evidence to close this guy down."

"Could it be more than one, sir?" Sanchez asked.

"There are several billionaires who built this thing, so it's definitely a possibility," Doc replied. "I can't believe if only one is actually poaching, the others aren't at least aware of what's going on. And if there are seals, then there could be other animals we don't know about."

Lee continued. "Tomorrow we'll be at Pearl getting our wardrobes and any equipment ONI believes we'll need. The day after, we'll be on one of the shuttle flights heading out to the resort."

"Damn, Captain, they believe in action, don't they?" Bates commented.

Doc sighed. "We have to save the seals that are left."

Andrea stood up. "We'll be ready, Doc, Captain."

Lee nodded. "I know you will. Everyone get some sleep. Mister Macon has already rearranged the schedules."

Just before he walked out of the small lab, Doc stopped him. "Be careful, Lee."

"I will."

Chapter Eighteen

Two days later, the COB and his lovely wife, Andrea Bates, took a charter flight from Kilauea. They checked into one of the cheaper rooms of the South Winds Luxury Pacific Entertainment Hotel. Lee and Petty Officer Maria Sanchez flew down on the same flight. They checked into a room under the name of Hawk. Mr. and Mrs. Hawk.

A major wildlife organization footed the bill, which made Doc happy because even the cheap rooms weren't cheap. Lee knew the government donated to the cause, too. Roger Rollings hadn't made many friends stateside when he left some big investors high and dry.

As Lee walked into the opulent fifth-floor room, he gazed at the gigantic television covering most of one wall. He slipped a tiny device, appearing like a car key, out of his pocket to check for spying devices. They had planted a bug in the TV. Not just listening, but viewing devices, too. He bet some of the hired help enjoyed interesting nightly entertainment.

He might as well begin the charade. "I didn't come here to watch TV," he grumbled. Then he looked to see if he could pull the television's plug. No plug, they wired it into the wall.

"Dear, we'll get plenty of time to do 'other' things later," Sanchez cooed, playing it to the hilt.

Lee leaned close and whispered in her ear. "You are convincing."

Her cheeks flushed pink.

He grinned and said, "Indeed we will. We're here for three days and three nights. Let's go out on the balcony and enjoy the Pacific breezes."

His cabin on *Sea Dragon* could fit twice on this balcony. There were several comfortable, all-weather chairs and a table with an ice bucket chilling a bottle of champagne. "Nice," he commented. No devices, but he couldn't be too sure about the strength of the one installed into the television set.

He pulled a chair closer and motioned for Sanchez to sit down. "Let's take a load off." As though whispering sweet nothings, he leaned close to her ear. "TV not only has a listening device but video."

"Yes, sir," she replied, also in a whisper.

"We're married, remember?"

"Oh…."

Lee popped the cork on the champagne and poured some into two crystal glasses. "To us!" he said in a jovial voice.

"To success," Sanchez added in a softer voice.

"Relax." He took a sip, then put the glass down. The balcony overlooked a larger than Olympic-sized swimming pool. Girls in skimpy bikinis partied with muscled men. There were also a few families with children and several retirement-aged visitors. Another pool contained water jets and slides. Most of the kids hung out there.

The sun shone in his eyes and Lee closed them, enjoying the combination of soft breezes and the heat of the sun.

Sanchez's hand on his shoulder woke him. The sun lowered into the ocean. "I can't believe I fell asleep," he muttered.

"I got really comfortable, too," Sanchez replied.

"Let's strut our stuff."

She nodded and went into the room to change for dinner. Lee stayed on the patio for a few minutes to give her time to put on her evening gown. When the bright orange and red sunlight faded into soft velvet blackness, he got up and slipped into the room, closing the door behind him. Sanchez was still in the bathroom, so he opened his garment bag and pulled out a borrowed tuxedo. He grimaced. These monkey suits were several steps below dress blues and he disliked wearing those, too.

He hung his tux up in the expansive closet. Sanchez stepped out of the bathroom. "Nice!" he gasped. A sequined dress showed off every curve of her body, with narrow shoulder straps keeping it morally decent.

She smiled. "Thanks! Could you zip me up, s—Lee?" She turned and her bare back looked just as perfect as her covered front.

"With pleasure." He zipped slower than necessary, then headed into the bathroom to get ready. He shaved and put on the tux, feeling uncomfortable about having no weapons. The liaison officer told them South Winds used enough security to make the Secret Service jealous. The government only required the team to find out as much as they could about the owners' clandestine activities. Then they would high-tail it back to the *Dragon* and report.

Lee knocked on the door at the end of a wide hall on the sixth floor of the hotel. Whoever built this place—the entertainment complex, swimming pools, helicopter pads—

had spent an obscene amount of money. They even gilded the door frames.

The door opened just enough for Bates to gaze out at him. "We're almost ready for dinner, uh, Lee."

"Maria and I will wait by the elevators," he replied. Bates nodded.

A few minutes later, Chief Bates and his wife joined them, and they rode down together. No one said anything other than basic pleasantries. Zuved brought the bug detector, discreetly hidden in his jacket pocket. He felt it vibrate several times.

The elevator opened directly into the restaurant. Lee's jaw dropped. Tropical plants in jewel-studded gilded pots lined the pathway to a fountain of water changing colors as it danced toward the ceiling. A short wall tourists could sit on surrounded the pool. While he watched, an older woman threw coins into the pool. Someone on the other side did the same. There were statues everywhere of mermaids, sea gods, and Polynesian royalty. All the statues seemed to be dipped in silver or gold and adorned with garnets, topaz, sapphires, and other precious gems. The Polynesians had cloaks covered with various colored feathers.

A maître'd in a black tuxedo met the foursome. His gaze fell on the two women and lingered there for a moment. Several other guests at nearby tables turned to check them out as well. Lee felt like a thoroughbred at the Kentucky Derby, having his pedigree checked out.

"Ladies, gentlemen. If you will follow me." The maître'd led the four of them to a table near a patio door.

Lee noticed the floor inlaid with what appeared to be metallic highlights. A huge chandelier hung from a beam in the center of the dining area. The crystals sparkled and light reflected on the floor. The partially open windows allowed them to hear the sounds of a South Seas band. While not as fancy as the maître'd, the band members were dressed in white tuxes. The music resembled classical with a South Seas flavor added.

Lee studied the menu. He kept a passive expression and felt for the expense card inside his suit jacket.

"I'd like the butterfly shrimp and lobster," Maria said first. "Even the sauce sounds heavenly."

Andrea Bates had a thoughtful look on her face. "I think I would like the sushi combo. I love sushi."

Lee did some mental math. *Six hundred dollars?* He shrugged. *What the hell…* "I am in the mood for coconut shrimp and stuffed crab."

Bates rubbed his chin. "You know, the South Seas platter contains what you want and the main thing I want."

"The seared flounder or the calamari?" Lee asked.

"Both."

"Sounds good to me."

The maître'd seemed to have radar, coming over to their table less than ten seconds after they had decided. He suggested several drinks to go with their dinners and Lee went along with the recommendations.

An hour later, he excused himself to use the men's room. A lame excuse to get away and snoop, but that's all he thought of. Lee didn't think he'd find a thing, but he had to check. He was right. This part of the resort was on the up and up.

With a sigh, he returned to the dining room. When the others glanced up at him, Lee gave a tiny shake of his head. He sat down just as the server rolled out the dessert tray. "You order first, Terrill."

Bates studied the cheesecakes, mousses, heavily frosted and decorated cakes. "Strawberry cheesecake."

"Bring me the mocha Tiramisu," Andrea Bates ordered.

"I'll have the same." Maria pointed to the Tiramisu.

"Mousse," he said. The server nodded and trundled off.

The group bantered while they waited. "We head out one at a time," Lee said in a low voice. "I will go out at two a.m. Maria at two fifteen. You and Andrea head out about two thirty and two forty-five."

"Where?" Andrea Bates asked.

"The marine area."

The others nodded.

"Your desserts, ladies, gentlemen." The server placed a plate in front of each one of them, then left.

"This is good!" Maria gushed. Andrea agreed.

Bates nodded. "This is delicious!"

He figured it better be, considering the seven hundred dollar price tag—including gratuities.

After a few minutes, Bates leaned forward. "There's got to be several acres of space out there, even past the marine exhibit pools."

"We see what's there, then get the hell out." Lee pushed the last of his mousse away.

He stood and pulled the chair out for Sanchez. "It's been a wonderful evening."

"Yes, it has," Andrea agreed.

Soon they were back in the room. "Too warm for blankets," Lee growled, tossing a comforter over the TV. He went into the bathroom to change into the dark clothes and gloves to camouflage him as he prowled. Maria did the same. He set his smart phone alarm and laid it under his pillow.

Lee turned out the lights. Despite feeling anxious, he fell asleep quickly.

Chapter Nineteen

The vibration of his phone woke him up. Lee tapped Maria on the shoulder and then stood up. Silencing his phone and stuffing it in an inner pocket, he also added a Swiss army knife and flashlight. Then he pulled out a small blue-tooth device that had recorded sounds. It would make any listeners think he and his 'wife' were having fun. He tossed it on his pillow.

He cracked open the door and saw no one in the hallway. Silently, Lee slipped out and strode down the hall. Instead of taking the elevator, he used the stairway. Outside, there were still some guests sitting around the pool drinking. Lee slipped behind bushes, unseen, keeping an eye out for any security personnel. So far, so good.

All the palm trees and large-bloomed hibiscus made great shadows.

A guard stood near the entrance, so Lee dashed along the enclosure, trying to find some place where he could slip in. He remembered the vague specs of this place and realized the other entrance would have a guard as well. There were no other entrances he knew of.

He saw a sign warning him about the electrified fence. Lee continued along the fence, hoping for a break, but figuring it would be unlikely. His frustration level soared, and he took several deep breaths to tamp it down.

Then Lee saw a tree leaning over the fence. He had never climbed a coconut tree before, but it hadn't looked too hard when he saw someone else do it. Remembering how they accomplished it, he grabbed the trunk, positioned his feet, shoes still on, and began climbing. At first, he got nowhere, then he made a little headway, inching along the trunk as it hung over the fence. The only noises he heard were the waves on the beach not too far away.

Lee sat on the tree trunk, gazing around, trying to spot Sanchez and hoping no one saw him. He didn't see or hear anyone. Letting himself dangle, Lee dropped the four or five feet to the ground.

The pools for the aquatic shows were empty. Most of them abutted to steep, forested hillsides. He studied the spectator area, noting its proximity to several block buildings. Heavy doors separated the pools and the spectator areas, but Lee didn't trust them. The obvious entrances were most likely the best defended.

Looking under the bleacher-like seats, he found an obscure doorway, which he hoped gave access to buildings. He tried the door and found it locked. Pulling out his Swiss Army knife, he opened a tool. Lee manipulated the lock pick apparatus inside the lock. Nothing. He tried another angle. Still nothing. Sitting back in frustration, he considered the lock. Digging the tool inside the lock again, he bit back a curse when it didn't work.

Lee turned on the tiny homing device only his team could pick up. Kneeling down, he checked the door again, testing the lock and the handle. The knife blade didn't have the strength to push the bolt out of the way.

He heard someone behind him and jerked around to see Maria. "Any problems getting here?"

She shook her head. "I helped the guard with his nap. He won't bother us." She pointed toward the door. "Let me try. I have something for recalcitrant locks."

Lee backed away as Maria pulled out a tiny devise about half the size of a remote control for a television. She held it to the lock and pressed a button. The device hummed for a moment, then stopped. Maria pulled out another device and, with her other hand, gently eased it in the door frame near the lock. The device hummed again and then the lock clicked. "Try it now, sir."

He did, and the door opened. He gazed at her in admiration and then studied her device. "What did you do?"

"A tech in the federal office gave this to me when we were briefing for the operation. He told me it might come in handy and he could only give out one. He called it a Loxi. It uses subsonic sound to work the tumblers. It moves them so I could slide the bolt open."

He nodded, all the while wishing he could have had one. "You'll have to show me sometime when we're back on the boat. Now where in the world are the Bates?" She didn't answer, and they waited a bit. "Let me go in and you wait another minute or two."

"There's been no alarms. Surely, they are coming, Captain."

"Something back at the hotel may have slowed them. We can't wait too long. Give them two more minutes and then follow me in—without shutting the door."

"Aye, aye, sir."

"Aye, aye, sir."

Chapter Twenty

Bates, watching from behind a bush, muttered under his breath at the people making their way to and from the main pool. They were loud, probably from the booze they were downing. He couldn't wait any longer. He stood up casually, as though he had been tying his sneaker, and then headed toward the aquarium.

"Where are you going?" a deep voice growled behind him.

Bates turned and saw a tall and beefy security guard. Sweat popped out on his forehead as he tried to think of a reason he would be out in his dark ninja duds, heading for a closed area. "Stepping out. To see a girl. Met her this afternoon."

"And you waited until two?"

"Uh, well. My wife…."

Beefy's eyes opened wide and then he grinned. "Light sleeper, eh?"

Bates nodded, and then shrugged. "She, uh, the girl, told me to come when I could."

"You're headed away from the rooms."

"Got turned around."

"She gave you her room number?"

"Of course. 1029."

Beefy pointed. "That building. Door on this side. Top floor."

"Thanks, man." Bates turned and trotted to the building. Yet another delay. As he approached the door, he looked for any other guards. None. The door opened quietly, and he slipped in, turning and looking for Beefy. The guard found someone else to talk to already. Bates slipped back out of the door.

Then he heard his wife talking to the guard. "I know you talked to my no-good skunk of a husband. I also know he's chasing a girl. Where'd he go?"

Bates snickered. She must have heard at least some of his conversation. He hoped the guard had no loyalties.

"Can you describe him?"

"Come on, come on," Bates muttered.

"Almost as big as you. He can't find his way out of a paper bag. I'm sure he had to ask directions."

"Uh, don't know where he went."

Andrea drew herself up. Not tall, she could still stand up to anyone. Her finger poked into Beefy's chest. Once, twice, and on the third time, the guard grabbed her hand. Bates bristled, ready to go to her rescue.

Then Beefy turned and pointed toward the building where he waited.

"About time," Andrea snapped. "What room?"

The guard told her, and Andrea stomped toward him. Beefy laughed as he walked away.

Andrea had almost reached the door when Bates called out softly.

Chapter Twenty-one

The door swung open to a wide entryway. When Lee reached a cross-corridor, he noted the width could accommodate animals, if need be. Like seals? He turned the small flashlight beam to the floor. He spied little dust, but footprints and cartwheels had smeared drops of liquid. It looked like blood.

Lee came to a stairway going down and stopped to decide his next move. He heard noise sounding like whales or dolphins–beyond the stairs, so he continued down. A muted blue light shone ahead of him. He slowed, not wanting to be surprised by anyone or anything.

At the bottom of the stairs, he found a glass wall at least three stories high, going one story down and one above him. Several belugas swam around, only stopping to check him out. One nudged the clear wall. Its eye gazed directly into Lee's. A narwhal and a couple of Pacific dolphins swam in front of the glass as well. They were fascinating to watch, but a noise above sent Lee back into the shadows.

Two men patrolled the catwalk along the top of the pool. They whistled, and the cetaceans rose languidly to the top of the tank. *Feeding time at this hour of the night*? He backed farther away.

When he reached the stairs, he met the other members of his team. Lee's relief brought a louder sigh than he wanted. "Any trouble, Chief?" he asked in a whisper.

"A guard stopped me out by the pool. Some guy with relations to King Kong," Bates began. "I made the excuse of stepping out on my wife."

Lee held back a laugh. "Sounds like a great story. I want to hear it when we're safely out of here." He pointed up. "There are a couple of workers above, so we're going slow and staying in the shadows. Be ready with your cameras and recording equipment."

They nodded and Lee led the way back down the stairway. Andrea Bates snapped pictures of cetaceans' mealtime. Then they took a corridor away from the pool. Lights were spaced farther apart. As they continued, the floor felt slick. When he shined his light on the concrete, it had a red sheen—even more than the corridor above him had. Lee thought he knew what might cause so much blood.

Chief Bates leaned closer and whispered. "You think this is what we're looking for?"

Lee nodded. The air wafting in his face felt warmer. "Be careful. I'm hearing machinery." They slowed even more. Ahead of them, the group heard a door opening.

"Let's take care of this before they bellyache again," someone snapped.

"It's heavy," a high-pitched voice whined. The door banged shut.

"Why do you think it has wheels? Shut up and push!"

The voices sounded closer. Lee's eyes searched for a place they could hide. He motioned, and they dashed back the way they came. Finally, he spied a slight bend and a doorway set into solid rock. If they squeezed together, they might not be detected. He motioned for the women to go in first and then he and Bates pushed behind them.

Lee sucked in his breath and released it slowly. Bates squashed against his wife, with his camera ready.

A worker whistled, while the other grunted as he pushed. The large cart came into view, piled high with what appeared to be fresh meat. Lee pondered what kind of meat it could be. The men concentrated on their task and didn't look toward them. Drops of blood oozed from the cart, splashing on squeaky wheels.

The men continued away and as soon as they were out of sight, Lee stepped out of the doorway and stared up the corridor.

"What was that?" Sanchez asked, wrinkling her nose.

Lee took a breath. "I think it might have been seal meat."

"What?" the women responded together. "Why?"

"Your idea about sealskin coats may have not been far off the mark, Terrill. And where better to get rid of the meat than to feed it to your zoo animals?"

"Disgusting," Andrea hissed.

"I agree. We need to get conclusive evidence so we can close them down."

"They're slaughtering endangered animals!" Maria looked ill.

"We've got to be careful. I don't know how long it will take the delivery boys to finish their meat run, but I doubt we have much time."

The group slipped along the shadowed side of the corridor until they reached the door the men had come through. He listened for any noise, then opened the door. The heavy scent of blood hit him like a slap. Lee also saw why he heard water splashing. This room opened to the sea.

Chapter Twenty-two

Lights shone overhead and the group could see everything going on. Seal skins were stacked near the entrance to the sea—one large enough for a small yacht to come and go. A dozen adult seals, mostly females, cried plaintively from a pen on the other side of the entrance.

Four men worked side by side, two of them skinning a recently killed seal and two heading for the seal pen.

"We can't let this happened," Lee hissed.

One man jerked up, shouted, and pointed at them.

"Scatter," Lee ordered. "Bates, you and Andrea try to let the seals out of the pen. Be careful. Sanchez, see if you can lock the door we came through and keep any unwelcome visitors out."

"Aye, sir."

He raced toward the closest man, noting the large skinning knife in his hand. Lee ducked and decked the man in a classic football tackle. He rolled away as a knife rattled out of his opponent's lax hand. The tall man lay unconscious where he fell. Another man came for him but approached more carefully, assessing his smaller opponent. Biceps bulged in his blood-stained shirt.

Lee grabbed the slick-handled knife and faced his opponent, who held a similar knife in one hand and a huge hook in the other. He swung the knife in an arc that would have taken Lee's head off if he had stayed put. The skipper ducked and reached in with his weapon, scoring a long bloody furrow down his opponent's leg.

The heavily muscled man cursed and leaped at him. Lee backed away, earning a few taunts from the larger man. He ignored them, concentrating on his defense. His feet slipped and he almost fell. His opponent took advantage of the opportunity, leaping for Lee.

Jumping sideways, the skipper slashed a long bloody furrow on the man's arm, and the hook fell from his opponent's numb fingers. It didn't stop him. With a howl of pain, the butcher grabbed at him, missed, and stumbled forward.

Lee kicked him in the side once and then twice. He felt winded, and the man grabbed his leg, pulling him off balance. His opponent smashed his fist into his side and then followed with a kick. Lee jumped out of the way of a second kick, despite his side sending sharp messages of pain. Then he stumbled over something laying on the floor. A quick glance showed him a club. He grabbed it. As the bigger man rushed toward him, Lee swung the club and dropped his opponent in his tracks.

He left the club on the floor and straightened up, one arm held tightly across his chest, the other hand holding the knife in front of him. The behemoth groaned and pushed himself from the ground, his knife still clutched in his hand.

"Drop it." Lee held the point of his knife closer to the man's throat. "Drop it!" The butcher followed directions and Lee snatched it up, adding to his knife collection.

Bates ran over. "You okay, sir?"

"Bruised ribs." He glanced toward the seal enclosure, finding it empty. Two other employees lay unconscious on the floor. "Nice job! You get pictures?"

"Got plenty," Bates answered.

Lee glanced around for something to tie the men up with and saw nothing. "Is there a room we can lock these characters in?"

Bates pointed to an open door. It appeared to be a small supply closet. "There?"

Lee thought he saw cleaning implements, a mop or broom hanging inside. "Tie them up if there's something in there. I don't want to fight our way out of here. Then let's get the hell out of Dodge!"

"Yes, sir!" Bates and his wife dragged the two unconscious men toward the little room. Sanchez herded the others.

Pulling out his communicator, he pushed a sequence of buttons, then shoved it back in his zippered pocket. When he straightened up, he felt muscles pulling and ribs protesting. By then, the others had returned. Lee motioned toward the ocean inlet. "I think it will be safer in the water rather than backtracking." Sharp pain ricocheted up and down his side.

Sanchez stepped to his side. "You sure you're all right, sir?"

He nodded. "Until Meyers gets a hold of me." When Lee looked out the passageway to the open ocean, he hesitated. There were several boats, all with headlights, and all facing the little inlet. They wouldn't be able to sneak away.

Lee turned back to his team. "They have the troops out." His breath hissed between his teeth as he tried to pull in a deep breath. "Three speed boats with searchlights." He studied the cavernous room, looking for another place of escape. He also hoped to find an arms locker. They could hold off the assault from outside for quite a while if they had weapons.

"Andrea, check the nearby lockers. See if there are any weapons."

"Aye, sir."

"Chief, barricade any other doors the enemy could come through."

"Yes, sir."

A short, narrow catwalk stretched above his head. There had to be a door up there somewhere. He climbed the stairs, holding one arm over his injured ribs. When he reached the top, he spied a small door unnoticed from below. Testing it, Lee found it locked, but it opened from the other side. There had to be a way to barricade it.

He studied the long and heavy knife in his hands. The links in the middle told Lee this was a swiveling meat hook. He pushed one end of the hook into the space between the door and frame. He hung the other end around the door handle. Then, with the handle of the second knife, he pounded the hook in as hard as he could manage. It would have to do.

"Found some weapons, Captain," Bates called out.

Lee shoved the other knife blade at the bottom of the door, kicking it for good measure. A couple of second's grace, but better than nothing. He sprinted back down the stairs and over to Bates. The cabinet held a half-dozen AK-47's, the same number of pistols, and some grenades. The latter would only be a last resort. "Let's take these and see if we can discourage the assault forces." He shoved a pistol into his waistband—away from the sore ribs—and grabbed the assault rifle Bates handed him. "Leave most of the grenades. We don't want to use those if we can help it."

"Yes, sir!" Andrea answered for everyone as she took her weapons.

"And I need someone to watch the doors in case someone gets through," he added.

Maria nodded and stayed behind. Lee found a narrow path leading from the room to the rocks at the entrance. Bates and his wife did the same on the other side.

The boats were cautiously maneuvering into the narrow channel. Lee motioned to the others. "Fire on the lights," he ordered. "But keep the boats out."

AK-47's were non-discriminating. Not only were searchlights blasted, but chunks of fiberglass and wood. There were shouts and the lead boat turned and revved up its engines. The others followed. Lee's group continued firing. The assault boats returned a few shots, one hitting the rock wall a few feet from his head and peppering him with gravel and dust. Lee ducked back and waited to see what they would do next. As long as he didn't move, the pain in his chest stayed a dull ache.

He felt a buzzing at his hip and pulled out the communicator. The sequence of tiny lights told him *Sea Dragon* remained a quarter of a mile offshore and Macon had dispatched a skiff in for them. Lee quickly sent off a message letting the XO know their present situation. More blinks. The skiff would come in silently and without lights.

The captain made his way over to the COB, updating everyone on the status of the submarine.

"So how do we get to the *Dragon*, sir?" Bates asked.

Lee had seen the dimensions of the speedboats and knew they were small enough to come right into the chamber. At least one at a time. If needed, the grenades would discourage that.

"Incoming!" Sanchez shouted, then fired at the door above them. They heard a scream, then the door banged shut.

"Nice work, Maria."

"I … I've never had to shoot a person before," she murmured.

"It's hard."

"I'll be all right, Skipper," she said after a moment.

"I know. Let's get out of sight from outside. We'll see how long it takes for someone to get curious again."

The group watched from behind the rocks as the boats bobbed on the water a safe distance from gunfire. Light glinted on the water from handheld flashlights. It didn't reach far, but far enough to keep the team from trying to swim out of the cavern. Five minutes passed, then Lee heard shouts from a nearby boat.

The captain felt the buzzing at his hip again, then heard a noise behind him. "The door!"

Bates fired a short round at each door. The door banged shut again. "Maybe they'll get the hint!"

Lee pulled out the communicator and translated the flashes. "A group from *Dragon* is causing a commotion out there." Screams and curses floated in from across the water. "We need to be ready."

His communicator buzzed again. "Let's go. Into the water. Our taxi's arrived." Lee took a breath and the stabbing pain reminded him of his disastrous fight with the behemoth. Bates fired off another round at the doors to keep Rollings' thugs at bay, then followed the skipper down to the water. Waves beat against the rock, saltwater splashing his face. Swimming and bruised ribs didn't go well together.

"Are you all right, sir?" Bates, swimming beside him, asked.

"I'll just be glad to be back on board." They swam to the opening to the sea. Then, over the waves, he heard the soft chug of an engine. *Theirs or ours?*

"Skipper! Chief!" a muted voice called over the waves.

"Here," Bates answered.

The rubber skiff eased over to them and an arm reached over to help them aboard. "Let me pull myself aboard," Lee said, then realized the impossibility of his statement.

Bates solved the problem by pushing the skipper aboard. He flopped to the bottom and tried to roll upright. "Damned ribs," he muttered.

"You okay, sir?" the sailor piloting the skiff asked.

At first, the pain kept him from answering. He kept telling himself he just had bruised ribs.

"Skipper did some tag-teaming with a gorilla in there," Bates said as he helped the ladies in and then pulled himself aboard.

"Any problems with the speedboats?" Lee finally asked.

"No, sir," Patterson said. "We came in silently and scuttled two of them, then the other took off. I don't think it went too far. Wildlife and Coast Guard have been standing by."

"Let's get out of here before anyone retaliates."

"Aye, aye, sir."

The trip to the *Dragon* turned out quiet and quick.

Chapter Twenty-three

Seaman Trenton helped him aboard and down the forward hatch. The XO waited for them. Macon checked him out with his eyes.

"Nothing serious, just got in a bit of a scuffle with the hired help," he answered the unasked question.

"Lee, you go get checked out. If you feel up to it, Doc is waiting for an update. He is especially interested in the pictures."

Suddenly, a rumble passed through the water, causing the boat to shudder.

"What..." Mace began.

"Explosion on the island," Lieutenant Brent, the officer on watch, declared.

Lee and Macon turned to the forward surveillance screen, set to night vision, and saw the side of a mountain they had just escaped from collapsing into the ocean. He couldn't see anything else exploding and hoped the hotel part of the island hadn't been affected.

"Getting rid of evidence," he muttered. Lee couldn't believe someone would destroy living creatures to save their asses. "Increase the magnification, Harris."

"Except you got pictures," Mace reminded him.

"That's slight consolation to those who were in the explosion." Lee studied the enlarged pictures. They had destroyed nothing else except the aquatic area. That was a relief.

"I hope this didn't cause any casualties at the hotel," Andrea Bates said, her eyes wide in horror.

"No," Lee said. "I'm only seeing damage on this side."

Macon shook his head. "Dammit, we can't go in and try to help in the event of casualties."

"If a call goes out for help, then we go in, Mace. I felt like an inadequate James Bond with no lawful authority in there."

"You were trying to stop a travesty, Lee!" Doc snapped from the forward control room entrance. "Why the hell do you think they blew up that section of the island? Where they did their environmental genocide!"

Chief Bates followed him in, so Lee knew Doc had seen the pictures.

"Rollings probably tipped the extinction scale for these seals."

Lee leaned against a console, slightly bent over, only wanting to get his ribs checked and take a heavy-duty Motrin. He also felt the weight of so much destruction.

Doc eyeballed the skipper. "Chief Bates told me you hurt yourself. Go see Meyers and we'll meet in the wardroom later. Bailey sent out an emergency call to the Hawaiian authorities. They'll take care of civilians and the conservation people will take care of the animals," Doc said.

No argument from Lee. In the tiny closet-sized cubby near the wardroom, which served as a Sick Bay, Ensign Meyers looked at the bruises, felt his ribs, and handed him an ice pack. When Lee just gazed at it, Meyers explained, "You have two cracked ribs as far as I can figure without an MRI. By the way, medical professionals don't use tape to treat cracked ribs these days. And until a couple of days pass, you need to take Tylenol for the pain, not Motrin. Then Motrin will be fine. Nothing strenuous, no lifting. If it hurts, don't do it. Use the ice as frequently as you can."

Lee nodded. "Thanks, Eric."

"No problem, Captain. If the pain gets bad and you have problems breathing, come back and see me immediately."

"All right."

Lee headed the short distance to the officer's wardroom and grabbed a cup of brewed cacao. Doc Wilson sat at a table, gazing at his iPad. Lee didn't think a frown could get deeper, but it did.

"What's the matter with some people?"

"Rollings?"

"And his backers. He couldn't do this alone. Especially, and be able to keep this much secrecy."

Lee sat down next to him. What showed across the iPad screen were the pictures the Bates and Petty Officer Sanchez took. Some figures and statistics ran across the screen as well.

"Have they tipped the scale?" Lee asked. After infiltrating the island operation, he figured he wouldn't like the answer.

"In the wild, they have. I don't know if a marine breeding program, similar to what scientists have done with red wolves, would work with the Hawaiian monk seals."

"They have to try, don't they, Rick?"

"Of course they do." Doc stared at the screen for a few more seconds, muttering. "That bale held almost fifty intact skins. Fifty lost individuals!" He sighed, then studied Lee. "What did Meyers say?"

"Couple of cracked ribs." He held up the ice pack, then stuck it back under his arm. "My new friend for a while." He sipped his cacao, thinking. "So, does this information go to the local wildlife officials?"

"Them and several other agencies. These guys were poaching, sending illegal animal parts to other countries—at least as far as I have found so far—."

The mess mate brought over a plate of treats—cookies, brownies, slices of apple, and other fruits. Lee snagged a cookie and a small bunch of grapes. "Please give my regards to the chop."

"I will, sir. We'll have breakfast in an hour and a half."

"Thanks," Lee replied. He shifted the ice pack as he turned back to Doc. "Let me know what I need to do."

"Get the reports to me as soon as possible. I want to nail this guy and his cronies."

Chapter Twenty-four

After a week of reports, sworn statements, testimonies, and discussions with several government agencies, *Sea Dragon* received clearance to leave. But where the hell would that be, Lee wondered? He hadn't heard from any of the places they had checked out.

In the meantime, Roger Rollings sat in jail, while a contingent of ten lawyers tried to get him out on bail. Lee didn't doubt he would disappear if they succeeded. As to Rollings' partners, they had already disappeared, scattering like cockroaches in the sudden light. The one who stuck around, a short little multi-millionaire, claimed he didn't have a clue about the activities inside the mountain. The feds couldn't find anything to disprove his claim. *Slippery like eels.*

The sub headed back to San Francisco. Lee slipped on his boat shoes and felt a slight pull in his chest, reminding him that while his ribs felt better, strenuous activities were still a no-no. At least he had lost the ice pack.

"Skipper?" The communications officer called.

Lee grabbed the intercom. "What is it, Henderson?"

"Call for you or Doc."

"From?"

"Well, sir, several places, but I think the one from the naval base in Seattle is personal for you and Doc Wilson."

Lee furrowed his brow, wondering. "I'll take the Seattle one first. Ask the others if they can hold."

"Yes, sir." Henderson handed him a headset.

"Captain Zuved?" He heard a woman's voice, someone he didn't know.

"Yes, ma'am."

"I am Marilyn Fuller. Admiral Drumwright's niece. I wanted to let you and Doctor Wilson know my uncle passed this morning."

Lee felt sucker-punched. He had grown close to the crusty admiral during their time together on the *Sea Dragon*. "Thank you for letting us know. Please extend our condolences to the family."

Doc stood nearby when Lee finished the conversation. "Admiral Drumwright?"

Lee nodded. "I'll let the crew know."

They both stood quietly for a moment.

"Captain? Doc?" Henderson asked. "There are two other calls waiting to speak to you."

Lee sighed. "Whose came in first?"

"I think the Juneau one, but they hit the 'wire' at the same time."

"Let me talk to Juneau. Doc, you take the other one."

Lee donned the headphones. "*Sea Dragon*," he answered. "Captain Lee Zuved."

"Captain Zuved, how wonderful to talk to you. We've spoken before. I'm William Bentley, head of the Juneau port authority."

"Yes, I remember our meeting, Mr. Bentley. What can I do for you?"

"I could be crass and tell you to bring your wonderful submarine up to Juneau to headquarter here." He laughed. Lee waited. "Seriously, the committee met and we would like to extend an invitation for *Sea Dragon* to use our port for your docking needs."

"Thank you, Mr. Bentley. I will certainly discuss it with Dr. Wilson and others involved in *Sea Dragon's* missions. I'll get back with you soon."

"Oh, and the committee felt it would be fair to waive docking taxes for two years."

"We appreciate it. I will mention your generous offer to Doctor Wilson, too."

"Thank you, Captain."

When he signed off, Lee noticed Doc on the other headset. He waited, checking the systems with the duty officers. Then he informed the ship about Admiral Drumwright. Because of the admiral, this one LA class boat gained a second life. Wilson finished and motioned for Lee to join him in his office. They had barely sat down when someone from the galley brought them a pot of coffee. Lee poured one for Doc. "Bring me some cacao."

"Yes, sir."

"Well, who did you talk to? Must be important if you wanted to meet here." He stretched out his legs, relishing the extra room of this converted area of the boat.

"Guam. They offered us a docking berth at Apra. And I hear Juneau called as well."

Lee nodded.

"So, which one should we choose?"

He took a sip of the steaming cacao, then blew on it. "Why not both?"

"Both?"

"Sure. Guam is about ten or eleven days from the states, but in all other aspects, it's close to many areas we'll be studying. Juneau is north and several days from the lower forty-eight, but it gives us proximity to the polar cap. Your scientific buddies are studying the hell out of the Arctic. Juneau would be close to that."

"Knowing our luck, we'll get a call from Puerto Rico and you'll tell me to take it, too."

"Why not? We don't have to build a base and houses, we just use what's available. I would suggest Puerto Rico as the primary base…. Cheaper cost of living and we'd boost their economy."

"If they call us."

"And the others would be auxiliary bases."

"Like a time share?"

Lee laughed. "Why not, except let them battle on who can make us the best deal. Our first voyage provided wonderful PR."

In the end, Puerto Rico called and *Sea Dragon* based out of San Juan, with berthing rights in Guam and Juneau. The submarine turned heads anytime she came to town and the city fathers were perfectly happy to have something else to brag about.

Chapter Twenty-five

Morley Trenton, Seaman, enjoyed the short time he had in the Turkish port. He enjoyed checking out the local outdoor market for souvenirs to send the folks back home in Tennessee. While serving on the scientific sub, SSRN *Sea Dragon* was a significant change of pace from a ballistic submarine, it was still a sub. A body hankered for fresh air and unfamiliar faces. Trent—no one called him Morley and left the room on his own power—stopped in front of a local coffeehouse. The brew smelled strong, like he liked it, but he had no time now. He looked at his watch. In an hour he had to return, and it would take him that long to find gifts.

Trent studied some skirts and shawls—bought one of each for his older sister, Claire. He found an Aladdin style lamp for his folks. Dad would get a kick out of it. Then he found an evil eye wall hanging for his younger brother. Someone made this one from Papier Mache painted bright blue with a small, white-rimmed hole in the middle—the evil eye so common in this part of the world. Devin would either laugh or run in terror at the garish decoration. Next, Trent picked out a doll dressed in a Turkish costume for his younger sister, Janeel. Undoubtedly, it came from China. When he turned it over and checked, it turned out to be locally made. The seller talked to him in Turkish. Probably telling him the same thing he had just discovered for himself. Trent frowned at the price tag. He wanted the doll, but he didn't have a heck of a lot of money to spare.

"Eighty lira is too much," Trent said, moving his hands to emphasize his displeasure. Actually, about ten dollars wasn't a terrible price, but it never hurt to save some money if he could.

The merchant continued telling him something. Trent didn't know what had the older man peeved. Probably his desire to quibble rather than just handing money over. Trent put the doll down and started walking away.

"Wait," a small voice said.

Trent turned around and saw a boy, about seven years old, dark eyes, thinly built, gazing at him. "Wait, please."

Trent waited.

"Sister make doll. Very good."

Trent nodded. "Sixty lira."

The merchant turned purple, but the boy spoke up quickly. "Eighty lira and this nice basket. Basket well made. Mother made it. Will hold many things for long time."

Trent considered. The way the boy held it, the basket already contained something. "What's in the basket?"

The youngster, who reminded him of his younger brother, Devin, glanced down at the basket and then back at Trent. "You come from boat? Big boat? Under water."

"Yes, I'm from the submarine—big boat." They had problems finding a deep enough slip and moored out in the harbor.

"This is good for boat. Save good things to eat."

Trent smiled. Turkish delight? Sounded good. "All right. The doll and the basket." He handed over the Turkish lira.

The boy quickly stuck the doll in the basket. Then he handed the basket to Trent. "Good. Thank you. Enjoy trip." The boy waved goodbye. The merchant bowed and said something in Turkish.

"Thank you." Trent bowed. He continued through the crowd on his way toward *Sea Dragon* until he reached a less crowded area. He might as well get some use from the basket and put the stuff he had bought inside. Sitting on a bench, he opened the basket and almost fell off the seat. A golden-eyed face gazed back up at him, phenomenally long whiskers folded back against the feline's body. The cat had smoky gray fur, lighter on the front paws. Not long enough to be Persian, but longer than a regular short hair. The face, while a little bit flat, certainly didn't have the squashed in look as a pure-bred Persian cat. In short, Trent now owned a beautiful cat, but it had no place on a submarine.

"Meow," it said politely.

Trent couldn't believe his turn of luck, even while pleased at the cat's demure manner. Still, he couldn't take the cat on board *Dragon*. Just as he reached in to pull the cat out, he felt a tug at his sleeve. Putting the lid back on the basket, he turned around, expecting some beggar. The pint-sized merchant wonder stood before him. He had a guilty look on his face. *He should.*

Before Trent could say anything, the boy spoke up. "Please, sir. Not trying to trick you. Trying to give good home to Dihana. She is good mouser. Boats need cats."

"A submarine doesn't."

"Please. Had to find new home. Have other cats. Father says no more. Cannot feed many cats."

"I can't take her on my boat."

A tear trickled down the boy's face. Trent didn't know if the boy's tears were genuine, but he felt his empathy switch turning to the 'on' position. He sighed. The XO would have to let him send her home when they got back to the states. Maybe he could find another sucker on the way to the boat. *Maybe pigs could fly, too.* He remembered the chop, Harris, griping about finding some supplies chewed and mouse turds on the shelves. Apparently submarines sometimes had vermin, but how would the officers feel about a biological rodent catcher?

Now the tears ran freely down both sides of the boy's cheeks. *The boy really likes the cat, and I'm still a sucker.* "All right. I'll see what I can do."

The boy's sad eyes glowed, and a huge grin lit his face. "I know you good American."

"A gullible one," Trent muttered. "What's her name?"

"Dihana. Like Dihana Prenzess."

"Okay. I have to get back to my boat. I can't be late."

"Thank you, thank you, thank you." The boy reached under the lid quickly and touched the cat, who gave a tiny meow. Then he disappeared, lost in the crowd.

Trent put the souvenirs in with the cat and closed the lid. He only had a short walk to the waterfront where a local skiff waited to taxi him and others back to the *Dragon*. He saw absolutely no one he could entice into taking a cat.

So, he climbed into the skiff, carefully holding the basket in front of him. Thankfully, the cat said nothing. Trent sat on the narrow seat across from a couple of his shipmates.

"You got goodies for the family?" Mac Wilson, a Petty Officer in the Engine Room, asked.

"Yeah. They like it when I bring little things or send souvenirs home. My younger sister is getting a pretty good collection of dolls from around the world. Believe it or not, Janeel asked for a cabinet to put them in last Christmas." Dihana continued to be quiet as their water taxi chugged across the harbor. She said nothing as he climbed on deck and checked in with the Officer of the Deck, Lt. Jg Joe Morales.

As he climbed down through the hatch, Trent wondered about his choices now. The only thing he could do—go find Harris. He laid the garments on his bunk, along with the doll and the lamp. Dihana mewed softly and tried to nuzzle his hand. There were a couple of shipmates sleeping in their bunks, so he said, "Shh!" and closed the basket.

She gave a muffled, 'Mrrff,' but the cat didn't make any other noise.

Trent made his way aft to the mess. He didn't see the chop or the chop's assistant.

Mac swigged on a cup of coffee. "What did you do, buy the basket to sneak out extras from the mess hall?"

Before he could answer, they both heard muffled cursing in the storage area. "Damned rats!"

Something banged and then something else fell and hit the deck. Trent had totally forgotten the basket in his hands. The cat pushed open the top and leaped onto the table. Mac gave a muffled cry, almost spilling coffee in his lap. Dihana jumped to the floor and then crouched at the doorway to the compact storeroom. After a quick sniff, she disappeared into the room.

Harris, the head chop, nicknamed Cookie, suddenly dashed out of the storage room and shut the door behind him. "What the hell just went in there?"

Something clattered off a shelf, then silence.

"Go ahead, Trent, you tell 'im," Mac said with a big smile.

Trent peered into the basket where he saw only the blanket the cat had been laying on. "Well, Cookie…."

"Did you bring a cat on board?" the cook asked, staring at the basket and then at the two men.

"Uh, well, Cookie…."

Mac laughed. "Just say yes, and then explain why you were mentally demented enough to bring a cat on board. And then how you're going to keep the XO, the skipper, and Doc Wilson from finding out?"

"Uh…"

"You already said that," Harris deadpanned.

Trent gulped and began, "I thought I had just bought a basket and a doll, but this kid told me his father demanded he get rid of the cat."

"And you were just the sucker to take it," Mac said, still chuckling.

Cookie shook his head, and they all heard a light scratching on the door. "I guess I can't keep it in there all the time." He opened the door and out of the shadows stepped the fluffy gray cat, a dead mouse in her jaws. "Whoa! It sure is fast." Cookie reached for it, but the cat gave a small growl and stepped back into the dimly lit storage room.

They could hear more soft growls and then the sound of crunching.

"Okay, tell me about this amazing rodent catcher!" Cookie demanded, pouring himself a cup of coffee. He sat down with Trent and Mac while the cat finished her repast in the storage room.

Trent told the two men the entire story. "I kind of hoped I would find someone who would want a cat, but I got the stink eye from everybody. I couldn't just dump her either."

"Well, I'm happy. Never had rodents on a sub before, but there had to be a few in the last load we picked up," Cookie said. "I don't know what Captain Zuved and Mr. Macon are going to say."

"Yeah," Trent said glumly.

A couple of crewmen walked in and grabbed some coffee and donuts.

"Who died?" Patterson asked, sitting down next to Trent.

Trent just shook his head. Then Dihana ambled out of the storeroom and began taking a bath under his table.

"What the hell?" Pat asked. "Where did the cat come from?" He reached down and wiggled his fingers. Dihana licked another part of her body and reached up to sniff the extended digits. She rubbed against Pat's hand. "Friendly isn't she?"

"Very," Trent replied.

The intercom announced the *Dragon's* departure. Trent didn't have duty for another two hours. Mac did, though. "Let me know what happens down here."

"Cookie, what am I going to do?"

"She's earning her keep. For right now, I'll keep her down here. Fix her up a bed and litter box in the storage room. I already griped to the COB about the infestation, but she's a pretty good mouse catcher. She may take care of the problem before Chief Andrea has to requisition any mouse traps."

"Will you?"

"Sure, but eventually you'll have to 'fess up.'"

"I know. Hey, I'll leave the basket and blanket. It'll be a good bed for her." The cat licked herself and then started rubbing ankles. Trent scratched behind her ears.

"What's her name?" Pat asked.

"Dihana, as in Dihana Prenzess," Trent said, imitating the boy.

Everyone sat quietly for a moment, then Cookie laughed. "That's too funny."

"What?" Trent asked, confused.

"Diana Prince? This cat is the Turkish equivalent of Wonder Woman!"

Even Trent smiled. "I'll go down to the machine shop and get a box and some of the litter they use for oil spills."

Cookie picked up the cat and took her back into the storage room. Trent followed with the basket. Dihana sniffed it and then prowled the darkened room. She growled but didn't come out with any mice or rats. After a while, she jumped into her basket, curled up, and fell asleep.

"Go get her a litter box. Let's get well underway before we let the XO know about our latest crewmember," Cookie said.

Chapter Twenty-six

Three days passed and Dihana stayed incognito to most of the boat's complement. She kept to herself, hiding and prowling in the storeroom when the crew came in for something to eat. Still, the scuttlebutt got around through the ranks of the enlisted.

Trent came and visited whenever he could, brushing her and cleaning her litter box. After the first couple of days, there were no rodents for the cat to catch, so Trent fixed Dihana bits of fish and beef. He noticed her getting rounder and wondered if he should back off, but he didn't feed her much. He continued giving her both meats.

A week into their research in the Mediterranean Sea, Commander Macon ambled into the mess to get a bite before retiring to his cabin. Trent had just finished cleaning out the litter box. He walked out with the bag in one hand and Dihana's dish in the other. When the XO walked in, he almost fainted. "Uh, good morning, sir." The officers rarely came into the crew's mess.

Macon glanced at Trent's hands but said nothing about it. "Good morning, Trent. I would ask what in the world you have, but since I am very familiar with the ritual of a litter box,

I won't. In case you're wondering, I came down to check out the rumors."

"Uh, sir?" Trent gulped and then gulped again.

Dihana walked out through the crack Trent had left in the storage room doorway. She sauntered up to the XO and wove around his ankles. Trent thought she looked obese. "Sir, I can explain…."

"Nice cat. Do you have a place for her to have her litter?"

"What, sir?"

"Litter. As in kittens. She's going to have babies."

"Kittens, sir?"

"You didn't know she was pregnant?"

"Uh, no, sir. I just thought she was getting fat on the extras we fed her to supplement the rodents she'd caught."

Macon laughed. He reached down and felt Dihana's belly. The cat growled softly and backed off, giving him a reproachful eye. "She's pregnant, and it won't be long before she gives birth. Where's she been staying?"

Trent showed him the basket.

"Probably not big enough, but you never know."

Cookie had just come in from the trash disposal room. When he walked into the mess, he gaped at Commander Macon. "Hi, sir," he stuttered. "Did you want me to fix you something for breakfast?"

The XO shook his head. "No, we're discussing the need for something bigger for this cat to have her litter in. And by the way, I have suspected for the past couple of days."

"You have, sir?"

"Yes, but I haven't mentioned it to the skipper or Doc. The skipper claims he doesn't like cats. Wouldn't want him to stress." He smiled, but Trent only felt sicker.

"She has gotten rid of all the mice, sir," Cookie said. "She's even taken care of the bugs."

"An excellent job, too. What's her name?"

Trent told him.

Macon reacted the same way Harris did. The object of his laughter jumped into his lap and started kneading. "By the way, other than checking to make sure everything is okay with mother and babies, I wouldn't bother her too much. She might get nervous and start moving the kids around. We wouldn't want her taking them down to the torpedo room." He rubbed her chin, and she began rumbling. "My mother and grandmother loved them and had several at a time."

"Thanks for the help, sir," Trent said with relief.

"No problem, gentlemen. I'll check on her occasionally, too."

"Thanks, Commander. I like cats, but don't know a lot about them."

"Tell me how you got her."

Trent told him, ending with, "I planned to have her shipped to my mother and dad after we were stateside again."

The XO nodded and smiled. "As you were, Seaman Dihana."

The cat meowed and licked a paw.

Chapter Twenty-seven

Dihana disappeared two days later, her food dish left untouched. Cookie looked around the storage room but saw no evidence of a cat or a litter of kittens. Trent searched in the crews' sleeping quarters, offered to clean the officer's wardroom, and poked around the back corners of the galley. No cat.

Trent began biting his nails again, a habit he gave up during his teen-age years. He thought of all the dangerous places where a kitten could get lost on a submarine. Cookie whistled a little louder, hoping it would bring his favorite assistant out of hiding.

Only the XO seemed unconcerned. "She'll show up," Macon said.

After another three days, she showed up, still fluffy, but much thinner. She meowed for dinner. The cook promptly chopped up a chicken breast for Dihana and laid it just inside the storage room door, along with a fresh bowl of water. He had to prepare dinner, but still kept glancing over to see what she did after finishing her dinner.

When he looked over for the tenth time, she had disappeared—like a puff of smoke. "Where the hell did she go?" he muttered.

By now, all the enlisted knew about the cat, as well as most of the officers and the scientists. Trent started a betting pool. The crew guessed the number of kittens Dihana had given birth to.

The second betting pool had everyone guessing who would find the kittens first. Where the mother had hidden her kittens was the third betting pool.

The XO laughed but handed over his three dollars to make three bets. He wrote all his guesses on slips of paper folded and put into empty cheese puff containers. They were kept safe by the COB. All the men, noncoms and officers alike, trusted Chief Bates.

***

For a week, everyone looked in dark corners whenever they had an opportunity, but no one found the kittens. Dihana showed up for grub and water, disappearing when she finished. The XO tried following her one evening, but just like the character the boy had named her after, this Wonder Woman had her own type of invisible jet.

Macon knew the kittens would begin exploring soon, and Dihana would have her paws full. He guessed four. When he felt her belly, he had detected four hard lumps, but there could have been more.

Another week passed without seeing the kittens. Macon was off duty, grabbing lunch in the wardroom, when he heard a quick blaring blast. It signaled a mishap. Macon grabbed the nearest communicator. "Report!"

"Smoke in one of the forward science stations. Top level."

"Get the fire crew up there on the double!"

"Already on their way, as is the captain, sir!"

"Anyone still in the room?"

"We'll know shortly, sir."

"I'm on my way."

"Aye, sir." Macon wove around the crews' bunks and the officers' berthing in record time. When he reached the laboratory in question, he saw Doc Wilson taking care of Dr. Maddie Olafson in another laboratory. The scientist had on an oxygen mask, still coughing. The fire crew donned their masks to go into the smoky room.

"Captain Zuved went in there a couple of minutes ago," Maddie choked out.

"What?" Macon yelped. "Why did he do that? He knows better!"

"He said not everyone got out," Doc said. "And before you ask, he didn't say who. Maddie told me no one had been in the room with her."

"Get the hell in there and rescue the skipper!"

"We're going, sir," one of the fire crew replied, his voice muffled in the emergency mask he had pulled on. When he opened the door, greenish smoke curled out. A second crewmember followed him and they shut the door behind them.

"What kind of gas is it?" Macon demanded.

"I'm sorry," Maddie moaned. "Some chemicals were too close to the burner while I ran experiments." She coughed. "I didn't watch closely enough."

"I don't believe it's toxic, but it's displacing the oxygen," Doc said. He glanced at the reinforced door.

As though on cue, it burst open and one of the fire crew half-carried the captain out.

"Lee!"

Gasping for air, the skipper held his arm across his chest. Macon wondered if the captain's ribs were bothering him again.

"Oxygen," the first crewmember called out.

Macon handed the canister over, watching Lee. The normally olive-hued complexion looked pale. Macon grabbed Lee's wrist and checked for a pulse. Good and strong. *Thank God.*

The captain gagged and hacked. Jackson placed the oxygen mask over his face and turned on the flow. Lee sucked in air. His color returned to normal.

"Lee?"

He opened his eyes and blinked. "Oxygen," he mumbled, grabbing for his mask.

Macon stopped him.

"No, give them oxygen."

"Give who oxygen?" Macon asked.

Lee reached into his shirt and pulled out a limp, fuzzy black and white kitten, laying it on his lap. He pulled out another one, gray like its mother, then another—this one darker, almost black. They were limp like the first one. "Give them oxygen. Where's the other one?"

The other crewman, Benson, laid a calico kitten on the skipper's lap.

Lee jerked off the mask and held a kitten up to the hose. Maddie kneeled near the captain and put her mask over another kitten.

"A box," Macon said. "We need a box with a lid."

"There's a large specimen box in there," Maddie said. "If it's safe enough to go in now."

"I think it is, but I'm still in my suit, Doctor," Seaman Jackson said. "Where is it?"

"Shelf to the left of the door."

Ensign Meyers dashed into the room, his first aid kit under his arm. "Anyone hurt?" He saw the captain and checked him over.

Jackson slipped in and came back in a minute. He put all the kittens in the box and pulled the mask off the hose of one of the oxygen tanks. Macon shoved the hose into a hole and shut the lid.

Jackson turned on the oxygen. After a couple of minutes, he lowered the flow.

Meyers studied Lee. "Get your mask back on, Captain. Your O2 level isn't up as high as it needs to be."

"Sure, Eric," the captain said with a weak smile.

"How in the world did you know the cats were in there?" Macon asked.

They heard loud meowing from the corridor. Dihana burst into the room, screeching to high heaven. She prowled around the box, trying to nudge the lid off. She pushed it up and started crawling in before Macon could check on the kittens. He continued to let the oxygen flow even as Dihana nudged and licked her babies.

Finally, Macon heard a tiny mew, then another. The calico groped her way to her mother and latched on. The others started moving.

Lee pulled off his mask. "How are they doing?"

Macon studied the kittens. "They look like they'll make it."

"They would have died if I hadn't gotten them," Lee argued.

"You could have died!"

"The last one. I couldn't find her."

"You even knew their gender?" Macon asked. "And again, I ask, how did you know about the cats?"

The captain shrugged. "Yeah, I figured out their gender. I may not have grown up around cats, but my dad's sister was the family's crazy cat lady. My sister and I spent a summer at her place."

"And…." Macon coaxed.

"I checked them out after they had spent some time in my cabin. They were born in my clothes cabinet. Dihana enjoyed the tidbits I brought her, so she let me examine her kids."

Macon laughed. "I'll be damned. Your cabin? I share the head with you. Did you know about the cat before she took up residence with you?"

Lee nodded. "I heard enough scuttlebutt to know we had a pregnant cat. One night, I heard a noise in my drawer. When I looked, Dihana had just delivered her kittens. Right on my clean underwear. That'll teach me to leave my door open."

Wilson laughed, and Dr. Olafsen giggled. Lee coughed.

"I thought you told me once you didn't like cats," Mace reminded him.

"People can change their minds." Lee peered into the box where the kittens had recovered enough to find the milk bar. He reached in and scratched under Dihana's chin. The mother cat licked her children, purring. Then she nuzzled Lee's fingers. "Of course, what's not to like about this brood?"

"So you moved them to the lab?" Doc asked.

"I did. They started making enough noise to keep me awake. I figured the lab would be safe, since few people used it, so I brought her here, found an empty cabinet, and propped the door open. Although, I am astonished she stayed hidden this long."

Mace shook his head. "Frankly, so am I. Meyers, are the captain and Dr. Olafsen cleared for duty? The kids and mom can probably go back into the storage room."

"No more fumes in the room, and Captain Zuved and Dr. Olafsen are in good shape. So are the kittens," Meyers said with a chuckle. "I'll do another checkup in twelve hours. And you know if either of you have breathing issues, headaches, or anything else out of the norm, come to me immediately."

"Sure thing, Eric. By the way, Mace, find out who won the betting pool," Lee added.

"I'll check with Bates. Oh, and just to let you know, Trent said he would ship Dihana and the kittens to his folk's home when we get stateside. Then we won't have to worry about them."

"Uh, uh. The kids can go to deserving families. As long as she's useful, Dihana will have a home on the boat," Lee corrected his XO. "And when she isn't, I'll take her home."

"You?"

"Me."

"I think Dihana made a cat lover out of you, Lee."

"Just tell me who won the bets."

"Aye, aye, sir," Macon said with a laugh.

Doc shook his head.

When Bates brought him the betting information, Mace understood why. Chief Andrea Bates won two pools outright and shared the winnings of the 'how many kittens' pool with two dozen other crewmembers.

Dihana promptly disappeared out of the science station with her brood. The rumor-mill said she went back to the skipper's cabin. The XO verified it several days later.

Chapter Twenty-eight

Lee sat on the corner of Doc Wilson's smallish desk in his equally smallish cabin. Commander Macon sat in the only other chair. Doc leaned back, a coffee cup in his hand. The *Dragon* lay serene in her berth in Puerto Rico, Roosevelt Harbor Naval station. Preparation for the next mission had already begun, although most of the complement still enjoyed leave for another two days.

The past five months had gone by quickly and, except for the Hawaii mission, pleasantly. Most of their picks for manning the *Dragon* had been right on target.

"I assume you brought us here to discuss our next assignment?" Lee asked.

Doc nodded, opened up his desk drawer, and handed a folder to the skipper.

Lee opened it and noticed a half dozen pieces of paper, including a map. As he read each one, he handed it off to Mace. "Antarctica. Ross Island. They want us to do several things at the same time."

"I will fly down ahead of *Dragon's* arrival," Doc began. "I'm meeting a team of scientists near Mt. Erebus where some of the strange radiation readings seem to be centered."

"We study shelf ice and take readings as we sail south," Lee explained, looking at Doc. "What theories exist about the radiation readings? According to this, it's fairly deep underground. Doesn't radiation occur naturally in some underground locations?"

"Yes, but not in this small an area or with such intense concentration. And if the volcano erupted on top of the source of the radiation, the gas release could be deadly, at least to places nearby."

"Places like Australia or New Zealand," Mace added.

"Exactly. So, *Dragon* is going to make all speed down to Antarctica, stand off Cape Evans, and wait for my communication."

"When are you flying out?"

"Two days from now, so I'll be here to help get the boat ready. We're not totally prepared for a polar excursion. I'll make the requisitions. You can pick some of this up in New Zealand." Doc sighed. "I envy you all. I would love to approach Antarctica from below."

"My flight will be roundabout, to Miami, Los Angeles, then to Wellington and down to Ross Island. It will take a little more than a day to get down there." Doc took a sip of his now cold coffee, grimaced, and put the cup down. "The crew is coming back aboard tomorrow, right?" At Mace's nod, he continued. "As soon as everything is in order, take her out."

"Okay, Doc. We'll get down there as fast as we can. I am guessing, between ten days and two weeks," Macon ventured. "Probably closer to two weeks since we have to pick up provisions in Wellington."

"I see docking permissions are already granted," Lee murmured, studying the notes.

He heard a small meow. Dihana jumped up on the desk, demanding attention. Her kittens had homes now with several of the crew member's families, and she had been spayed. She only grew plump from eating handouts—despite the edict to not sneak food to the cat.

Lee scratched under her chin, and Dihana started her engine.

***

When they got under way, Mace ordered the submarine to a one hundred and fifty foot depth at full speed. He only moderated the proscribed route in order to run a few safety drills. By now, the scientists were used to the various emergency drills—drills necessary to keep the submarine, as well as her crew, safe. They made it to Wellington in nine days.

Some crewmembers had never crossed the equator, so Macon arranged a crossing-the-equator celebration. The XO sat in the officer's wardroom, where Bates answered his summons for a meeting. The chief had a funny look on his face when he entered. Somehow, Mace figured Bates had caught wind of his request. "Have a seat, Terrill. Just wanted to ask you a favor."

With a nod, Bates sat.

"We have eighteen folks who haven't crossed the equator, and I'd like to invite them to leave the ranks of pollywogs and become official shellbacks. Besides, we've worked hard the past few months, and this is a good excuse for a party."

"Do you want me to plan the festivities, sir?" Bates asked.

Macon shook his head. "I want you to be King Neptune. A favor, mind you. Not mandatory."

"All for fun? No mean tricks?"

Macon wondered if any of his commanders had subjected Bates to some of the cruel hazing of the past.

"Absolutely no hazing. No one is even required to attend. The worst anyone will be subjected to will be the pollywog race if they choose to join in."

Suddenly Bates grinned. Macon remembered that one of the people on the pollywog list was Andrea Bates.

"I would be happy to, sir. Do I have to come up with my costume?"

"Of course! And in three days."

"Aye, aye, sir."

***

Three days later, Bates entered the wardroom, looking like a black Santa Claus. He wore a fake beard made of packing material. His broad chest was bare. He wrapped himself in a robe made from a red curtain. A small but sturdy table became King Neptune's "throne." It sat on one side of the officer's wardroom. Someone found a Burger King crown.

Most of the command crew, those not on duty, dressed as pirates, as did many of the sailors. Someone laid out a racecourse from the crew's sleeping quarters on one end to the wardroom.

Lee addressed King Neptune. "Mighty ruler of the seas. As captain of this peaceful ship, *Sea Dragon*, I implore our uninitiated pollywogs be spared the…" He gave a dramatic cough. "Necessity of crass initiation."

Neptune laughed and then shook his head. "No! Let the ceremony begin."

"Aarrh," yelled the pirates.

Lee took the microphone and called to the officer on watch. "Let the race begin!" For a few minutes, they only heard the sounds of Cookie and his crew in the back finishing up the goody trays.

But soon, there came the sound of laughter and the thumping of hands and feet. The herd of pollywogs, some dressed in decorated swimsuits, thundered on all fours into the wardroom. All the pollywogs had to walk the plank into a pile of packing materials and whatever other soft things the crew had pulled together.

"I, the King of the Seas, declare all pollywogs to be official shellbacks!" Bates shouted, then laughed heartily.

Cookie and his galley assistants set out a party, the likes of which Mace had never seen before.

Guac and chips, salsa, refried beans, egg rolls, pot stickers, Chex Mix, cookies, cake, and non-alcoholic punch. The party spilled out from the wardroom to the crew's mess. Even Dihana got into the act when a few peanuts fell on the floor and she batted them around. At least, she did until someone stepped on her tail, then she took off for the captain's cabin.

Chapter Twenty-nine

As the *Sea Dragon* approached the Antarctic ice shelf, Mace slowed the boat. They glided in some kind of fantastical, other-worldly landscape. The monitors picked up sheets of ice dimpled like golf balls.

"All ahead slow. And keep her at one hundred feet."

"Aye, sir. One hundred feet. Ahead slow."

The monitors picked up two leopard seals streaking past them, their spotted pelts a blur the cameras replayed in a slower motion. The long-range bow camera found the bottom littered with bright little sea stars, a stick-like sponge, and the sea thick with krill. Small fish wove among other growths. Sonar revealed many varieties of life.

Mace watched the cameras in rapt attention. Even after five months, this kind of view never ceased to amaze him. "Who would think there'd be so much life down here in this kind of environment?"

"Anti-freeze," Lee said with a laugh. He stood in the aft doorway leading down to his quarters. "Where were you in oceanography class? The Antarctic fish have antifreeze to keep them from freezing solid." He paused. "But I don't think I have ever seen so much krill. It's like a blanket!"

"No wonder the whales enjoy it so much down here."

They watched in awe. "Satellite maps aren't as accurate down here. Watch the sonar and hydrophone input," Lee admonished.

"Aye, aye. We're watching, sir," the chief of the watch replied.

The officer of the watch gave coordinates to dock twenty yards out from the tip of Cape Barne. The submarine only had a thin layer of ice to break through there.

"Bring her up slowly."

The officer of the watch repeated the order. The sub rose, while various coordinates were called out. Finally, there was a thump and a bump, some cracking sounds, and then a brief grating noise. Finally, "All clear!"

"Secure!" the watch called out.

***

Lee donned his layer of heavy arctic gear over his jumpsuit and climbed up the ladder after the Officer of the Deck. The sun shone through a crystalline fog, blue peeked out between light grayish clouds. "Try to call Doc at Erebus station."

"Aye, sir," the OOD replied and relayed the message to communications.

Sharp wind found its way down his neck, despite having the parka hood tightly tied. With the binoculars, Lee could see Cape Barne and a few buildings. He didn't understand why the rendezvous wasn't closer to the scientist's base. They could have punched through ice twice as thick as this had been.

He mentally shrugged as he continued to scan the area. The wind kicked up snow and ice pellets and didn't allow him to see if there were any people in those buildings. It didn't look like it. He studied Mt. Erebus in the distance, but clouds wreathed the volcano. After five minutes, Lee climbed back down, pulled off his parka, and headed for communications.

"Sparks, anything from Doctor Wilson?"

"Yes, sir. This just came in. For your eyes only." Sparks handed him a small piece of paper.

He thought just how few of the paper communications he had received in the recent past. Most messages these days came on the iPads or monitors. This must really be important. He read it twice. It sounded a bit cloak and dagger to him, but he would follow the directions because it had Doc's verification.

The XO stood nearby. "Mace, I am leaving you in command of the boat until I return. Have Chief Bates, Ensign Meyers, Ensign Henderson, and Chief Robbins report to my cabin on the double."

"Aye, Captain."

Chapter Thirty

Although tight, the five team members fit in his cabin. "I got a communique from Doc," Lee began. "He's at a hidden science station near the base of Mt. Erebus, the north summit. He wants me and Ensign Meyers to rendezvous with his designated contact near Hooper's Shoulder." Why in the world couldn't they just didn't meet with all the scientists at one time? "Chief Bates, if this chart is still accurate, we should be able to take the snow-cat to within a half mile of the rendezvous on Erebus. Then you will wait there for our return. Henderson, you'll remain on the *Dragon*, but you're going to have a dedicated communication line open to us." He stabbed a finger in the middle of the contour map. "Be ready to send someone out to help us in case something happens."

Margo Henderson gazed at the map. "Aye, sir, but it won't be quick."

"I know. But nothing should happen." He hoped.

"When are we going, Skipper?" Robbins asked.

Chief Robbins's qualifications far exceeded the rest of them for this mission. She had trained under Meyers in first aide and competed in cross country skiing events when she had leave. Robbins may look petite and genteel, but this was one rock-hard lady.

"Good question. The message came with an urgent label, so as soon as we are ready, we're going. It's oh four hundred hours now. The rendezvous with our contact is a short way up the slope—seven miles from our position. So, if we are ready within a couple of hours, we should be able to get there quickly and get back before sunset. I want you to supervise our readiness."

Lee continued, "Terrill, you get the men necessary to pull out the parts to the cat and put it together. Give me a report in an hour and we'll go from there."

"Aye, aye, sir." Robbins and Bates almost trotted out of the cabin.

"The cat is too small to bring more than one other person back," Meyers reminded him.

"We shouldn't have more than one other person. Doc is still at the hidden camp. Otherwise, the note only said we meet this person and bring him back to the boat. Also, the individual might need medical attention."

"Medical attention? I guess if he walked from their base on the north side."

Lee shook his head. "Hopefully, he had a snowmobile."

Within two hours, the group donned layers of survival gear, from the foundation layer to a mid-layer, to the down-filled outer layer. They climbed through the hatch and from there negotiated down to the broken ice, and to the snow cat. The heater barely kept the cabin warm enough to not see one's breath, but Lee's fingers and toes remained happy.

It was rough, but the cat negotiated the ice sheet, and then powered over ice-covered, frozen ground. Terrill Bates drove and Lee saw the intense concentration of trying to stay on the more level parts of the course. It amazed Lee how quickly the machinist's mates had put it together. There had been several larger pieces, medium-sized pieces, and all the bolts and screws to put it together. The ice and rocks caused the cat to bounce and buck, but it kept the icy wind out and got them close to the rendezvous site quickly.

Low, dark clouds scudded across the sky. Ice pellets beat on the plexiglass window and the sides, sounding like someone trying to pepper them with b-b pellets.

"How are you doing, Terrill?" Lee asked.

"So far, so good, Skipper."

They continued until the slope grew too slanted. When the cat struggled, He motioned for Terrill to halt the vehicle. "No farther, Chief. Meyers and I will walk from here."

"Aye, sir."

With little conversation, Bates and Robbins handed Lee and Meyers their gear. They were only supposed to meet someone, so they carried the survival supplies they might need in case of a delay on the slope.

By now, the snow ice combination blew fiercely. The goggles and thick gloves they wore insulated everything. "Sparks? Henderson?"

"Yes, sir. I'm standing by," came Henderson's voice over their communicator earbuds.

"Excellent."

"Good luck, Lee!" Mace's voice came over the communicator.

"Thanks!" Then he turned to Meyers. "Let's get this taken care of. I'm sure our contact will be glad to get out of this, too."

"Sounds good to me!"

They trudged up the slope, Lee consulting the compass and Meyers watching the path in front of them. The snow pellets thickened, and the wind increased until the howling permeated not only his ears but every cell of his body. Each team members carried a hand-held communicator, but Lee didn't dare pull his out right now. It would probably slip from his fingers. Thankfully, the precipitation didn't stick to his goggles. Too damned cold, he thought.

"Can't believe I'm climbing a mountain slope in the middle of Antarctica," grumbled Meyers. "I wouldn't be able to give first aid even if someone needed it. My fingers would be numb."

"As far as I can tell, we're close to the rendezvous."

As if someone had flipped a switch, the wind quit blowing. A thick fog curled up the slope and around their ankles like a sleepy cat and floated in pockets like quicksand. Lee didn't like the analogy. He stumbled, quickly recovered, and continued up the slope.

"You okay, Skipper?"

"Sure, Eric. Someone tell me why people want to live down here voluntarily."

"Beats me, Skipper. But this is just plain creepy." Suddenly, Meyers slipped on something, and fell, lost in the fog.

"Meyers! Eric!"

Lee slid a few feet, still calling. He heard moaning up-slope, as well as a voice on his headset, but he ignored both, more concerned about his CMO. "Eric! Where the hell are you?" Then, several feet away, he saw a hand raise out of the fog like something in a zombie movie. He carefully pulled Meyers to a sitting position. "What happened? Are you all right?"

"Oh, man, someone get the license…."

"Are you hurt?"

"Banged my head and my funny bone isn't laughing," Meyers replied.

"Let me go up to the rendezvous, and I'll come back down with our contact. Can you hold on out here until we get back?"

Meyers nodded. "Yes, sir, and I'll join you when everything quits spinning."

"No, you just wait here. Call Henderson, and then Bates, and let them know what's going on. It might help if Robbins came partway to meet us on the slope."

"Yes, sir. That probably is the better plan."

"Holler if you need help."

"Aye, aye."

Lee stood up, checking his bearings. They were almost at the coordinates Doc gave them. The wind moaned again—no, not the wind. Despite the moaning sounding like a person in distress, he slowed his march up the slope. He stumbled and almost fell. There would be no running. The light faded fast, or maybe the fog had thickened. Didn't the sun shine more this time of year? The moaning sounded closer.

Pulling out his flashlight, Lee noticed someone laying on the ground. The fog drifted away. He turned the shapeless mound over as gently as he could and realized he was looking at an older woman. She opened her eyes slowly, blinked a few times, and then focused on him.

"Are you Captain Lee Zuved?"

"Yes, I am."

"Dr. Wilson sent me to meet you. And to bring you a message."

"Let's get you to the boat first. It's too cold to stay out here, especially if you're sick or hurt."

"I don't think I can make it." She fumbled in her pocket, finally pulling out a piece of paper and handing it to him.

It had his name on the outside, resembling Doc's writing. He could read it when they returned to the cat. He stuffed it in his pocket.

"What? Of course, you can. We have a snow cat at the base of the slope. I can carry you. Let's get you wrapped up and you will feel better." He couldn't figure out why she had unzipped her coat.

She grabbed his wrist with her mittened hand. "No, listen. Let me tell you what you need to know. I am Dr. Susan Baker, part of a scientific team studying Mt. Erebus for the past few years. I am also dying of cancer. It's just sooner than I expected." She drew in a ragged breath and began coughing. Finally, she got control and continued. "My group of six scientists were working on the geological readings of Mt. Erebus. We stumbled on an extra-terrestrial spaceship and a hidden base. About two months ago."

"What?" Lee pulled off his mittens to get her coat zipped up.

She continued as though he hadn't spoken. "The spaceship crash-landed. They are trying to fix it, and have come close to finishing, but they need fuel. Most of the aliens are friendly, but I have to warn you about some of them. Some want to use humans as hosts." She gasped and choked, jerking at her mittens at the same time.

"What? What do you mean 'use humans as hosts'?" Lee wanted to make sure he heard correctly. "And are you the one who called Doctor Wilson down here?"

"The note…."

"It's too cold out here. Let's get to the cat."

Again, she ignored his urgings. "Some of them want to use humans in a symbiotic role. As hosts." She wheezed, coughed again, and then continued. "We sent for Dr. Wilson when we thought they were all on the up and up. With his expertise and influence, he would be invaluable in helping them." She took another breath.

Horror clawed inside. *Use humans, hosts*? "No, you make this sound like we're dealing with some kind of parasitic invasion force. No way in hell is an alien going to be running around inside my boat! Passing along germs or viruses."

"No, not parasites, symbionts. None of them would have considered using a species as intelligent as humans for hosts if some of their own hosts weren't dying. We've been around them for two months. Not caught anything. Give me just a little more time."

Baker tried to draw in enough breath, unsuccessfully. Her lips were blue.

"Let's get you back to the submarine." Lee had trouble with her zipper. Dr. Baker latched on to his wrist as though grabbing a lifeline. Her fingers felt icy. She had to be delirious. Eric could give her something for pain when he got down the slope. "Look, Doctor, let's get aboard the *Dragon* where you'll be warm and then we can talk more about these aliens and Dr. Wilson."

"Haliss did not want to use high IQ beings as hosts… even less interested in a human/kreon relationship now." She sagged and slid to the frozen ground.

Lee reached down to pick her up. What did she mean about this Haliss interested or not interested in a relationship?

"Please, Captain. Please listen to Haliss. She begs you to host her for a short time and she will explain. Listen…to…her," Baker gasped, her last breath escaping from between blue lips as she slumped in his arms.

Suddenly, a small creature looking like a rectangular pancake-sized piece of liver slid on her hand from under the sleeve of her thermal wear. Lee gaped for a second until it leaped on his parka. "What the hell?"

He drew back, dropped Dr. Baker, and tried to shake the thing off. But it wouldn't shake loose. He felt panic growing in his gut. The creature—alien—wriggled down to where he had pulled off his mitten. Lee lunged for it with his other hand, but just missed the tail-end as it slid inside his sleeve. How it got under the extra layer of clothes, he didn't know—he didn't care, he just wanted it off. Lee felt the coldness of the 'liver' flowing up his arm and tried to claw his parka off.

"Get off me, damn you!"

Chapter Thirty-one

In a frenzy, Lee undid the zipper and buttons, but the creature slid around his chest faster than he could get his parka off. It must have had some kind of little feet, maybe cilia, because it didn't feel 'slimy.' Instead, Lee felt light touches as it scurried across his skin. He moaned as he kept trying to reach it. Then it stopped right in the middle of his back.

Lee jerked off his parka and tried to reach it. He began pulling off the other layers. As he prepared to throw himself on the ground, to squash the alien, he felt blinding pain reaching upward into his head, down his spine, and through his body. His stomach churned and he retched. His mind had caught fire. He stumbled, falling on his hands and knees on the hard ground. The cold burned. His insides burned. Lee closed his eyes tightly, attempting to block out the creature's presence and the pain it caused.

<Captain Zuved. Captain!>

"Get it off, Meyers! Get it off!" he cried, thinking the ensign had caught up with him. The cold continued, an intense fiery cold not just from the Antarctic wind. It clawed inside his head, slid up his back. He cried out again, then moaned. A mind-numbing headache accompanied the bitter cold.

Someone spoke to him through his earbuds, but he couldn't understand them. Lee gasped, trying to draw in enough breath. The nausea overwhelmed him, and the bit of breakfast he'd eaten earlier came up.

<Captain Zuved. You must listen to me. Please listen to me.>

The voice spoke the same words over and over, sometimes calm and sometimes like orders from a drill sergeant. "Meyers? Robbins?" His ears buzzed, but Lee still couldn't translate the words flowing from the earbuds. They sounded like another language. He slowly opened his eyes, trying to ignore the flashing lights at the corners of his vision. Baker lay motionless on the hard ground next to him. He checked her pulse and confirmed what he figured before—she was dead.

"Lucky her," he muttered. Baker said she had cancer. She had cancer and an alien.

<Haliss.>

Lee shook his head, looking around again. "Get off of me," he groaned.

<I am Haliss, a commander in the Kreon Defense force.>

Lee jerked up and instantly regretted it. His head felt like a drum being played with a baseball bat. The voice didn't come from the air; it bounced around in his head! "Who the hell are you?"

<Dr. Baker explained a little about us. About my need to talk to you.>

"I want you off my body—out of my head!"

<We have made contact—are in the initial stages of synaptic connection. We will both die if anyone tries to remove me.>

Lee shivered more from the horror of what happened than from the Antarctic cold. "Attached to a thinking thing, without … a body."

<I am not an 'it.' I am Haliss.> The voice said airily. <I am a leader among my people. But it is a biological issue if any of your underlings try to take me off by force. We are inseparable for the moment. Sharing enzymes and nutrients.>

"Skipper!" Meyers called close by.

Taking enzymes and nutrients. How the hell can I get rid of it? "Meyers?"

"I heard you yelling and thought you were hurt. What are you doing with your parka off? You'll freeze."

"Meyers, I want you to go back to the cat. Leave me here. The creature said taking it off would kill me, so just leave me here and it won't get on the boat."

"What? What creature? I don't understand. What's going on?"

Lee took a deep breath and sat up straighter, still feeling his eyeballs move with the beat of his heart. He pointed to Baker's body. "She came with a parasitic, alien creature. It hopped on me when she died. So, you need to leave me."

<Symbiotic, Captain. I am a symbiont.>

"Skipper, I can't do that."

"It's an order!"

<Of all the obstinate creatures. Why in the white suns of the galaxy can't you listen to me? Dr. Baker didn't have that problem.>

"Because you forced your way on my body like some kind of leech and then into my mind, which I enjoy having to myself! Dr. Baker probably had enough medication in her system, she didn't feel the elephant dancing in her head."

Meyers gaped at him as though he didn't know what to do or say.

Lee tried to stumble to his feet. If he ran, fell, jumped into the volcano, anything…

The imperious voice boomed in his head. <Mercurius, hope, fidelius, Winston Churchill.>

Lee started saying something and then stopped. He glanced at Meyers's outstretched arm. "What did you say?"

"Take my arm, Skipper."

The alien repeated the phrase.

"How? Did you force Doc?" Lee stammered.

"What, sir?"

Lee waved Meyers off. "I'm talking to the alien." At the medic's bug-eyed stare, he continued. "I'll explain."

<You can think your comments to me. As to your question. I don't know if you'll believe me, but Doctor Wilson gave those nonsense words to me voluntarily before the Leadership sent me out with Dr. Baker. He specifically wanted me to find you and he said you would understand what I said.> Suddenly, Lee saw an image of Doc Wilson alone with Dr. Baker. Doc reached his hand up the inside the of Dr. Baker's blouse, but he realized Doc touched the alien.

<Haliss.>

Doc touched the haliss.

<My name is Haliss. I am a kreon. I told you before.>

Lee tried to digest everything through the pounding in his head. *Is touch the only way you communicate with other species?*

<Amongst our own, no. Amongst other species, yes.>

"What are you trying to do? Take over humans? Use us. Make us slaves? Nothing symbiotic about that. Sounds one-sided."

Meyers made some noises, but Lee ignored him.

<No! I am not trying to take over your people! We work with hosts, but your people are too intelligent, even if *you* don't

seem to be right now. Think your questions, please. I will explain our *symbiotic* relationship later.>

Lee took a deep breath, felt the cold air burning his throat. *I understand those words. It's a sort of secret code. But why? Why would Doc want me to cooperate with you? You have violated my space—my mind.*

<He felt you and your crew could find him as well as find a solution to this whole situation.>

"What situation? Does he have one of you riding shotgun?"

Haliss paused. <Do you mean is he hosting one of our people?>

Yes.

<No, he is not. At least not when I left with Dr. Baker. We spoke because he trusted me enough to touch me, creating a temporary bond.>

How did Dr. Baker get here? How could she walk so far?

<About forty of your yards away, there is a small machine. She drove it until she hit a boulder and couldn't go any further. Then she walked.>

Did Haliss force the doctor to walk the final yards to meet him? To find her next victim?

<I stopped using her limited nutrients from the time she left the science base. She came of her own volition.>

"How much influence can you exert over me?"

<Do you mean if I could control you and make you do things on your submarine to destroy it?>

"And destroy the crew." Lee shivered. The cold Antarctic wind had put out the fire inside his body and mind, but not the blistering headache. He shivered and suddenly couldn't stop.

"Skipper? Captain!"

Chapter Thirty-two

"Captain! Captain Zuved! Wake up! You can't go to sleep out here." Meyers felt everything going to hell in a hand-basket. What had the captain said? A parasitic alien attacked him, attached to him? But where? Regardless of what happened here—of whatever delusion the captain might suffer from—he had to get the skipper back in his parka.

Meyers didn't see any sign of trauma other than the cold. "Captain, I'm getting your coat back on. If you can help me…."

The skipper moaned, put one hand to his head, and jerked out the earpiece. Then he went limp.

"Damn it!" the chief medical officer shouted. Even with the captain's dead weight and violent shivering, Meyers pulled the coat back on and zipped it up. Hopefully, Captain Zuved would warm up now. Meyers slipped a hand warmer in each of Zuved's mittens before putting them back on. The captain still shivered, but not as violently. Then the ensign tied the skipper's hood.

Meyers glanced toward the woman who had brought them out here, and realized he needed to check on her, too. The captain said Dr. Baker was dead, but he also admitted to dealing with an alien. Meyers swore again. Leaving Zuved,

Meyers dashed up the slope as fast as his sore knee would allow and checked on the scientist. Her parka lay open to the elements. One mitten off.

What happened up here? While he pondered, his earbud went crazy with requests from Henderson back on the boat and Bates at the cat. They both spoke, and Meyers couldn't understand anything either of them said. When he looked down and saw his long-range communicator blinking, he realized why they were almost hysterical. "Oh, crap." Meyers had left it on and he could only guess what the two men heard.

Pulling out his communicator, Meyers took a deep breath. "Chief Bates?"

"What the hell is going on up there, sir?"

"I have a problem up here, Chief."

Bates sounded calmer than before. "What's going on?"

"The captain is unconscious and our contact is dead." Meyers reached over and checked Zuved. Still unconscious, but his breathing and pulse were good.

"Unconscious? You'll need both of us. We'll be up there as soon as we can." Bates said nothing for several heartbeats. "I heard some strange things."

To Meyers's ears, it sounded like they were already trekking up the mountain. "Uh, so did I, Chief. I don't know what to do about it, to be honest with you. Except get Captain Zuved back to the *Dragon*."

"We'll be there ASAP."

Then Meyers called the ship. The ensign promised to keep them up to date.

Chapter Thirty-three

Lee wished the guy with the sledgehammer would take a break.

<It is not healthy for you to remain out here. However, you need to see a bit of our people's background, and then you will understand the complexity of the answer to the question you asked. And please remember, you may think your questions.>

Lee groaned. He hoped everything had been a nightmare. *Speak in shorter sentences or, better yet, leave me alone.*

<The pain will subside. I am going to show you something from my memories. It will explain a lot.>

Lee felt himself floating in another place. It looked a little like the control room of a sub, but soon realized this was the control room of a spaceship. He felt anxiety clawing inside. Were they abducting him?

<This is from the past. Memories.>

Ape-like animals moved around, working controls in a manner not too unlike the routine on a submarine. He shoved his anxiety to the back of his mind. He might as well find out what he could in case of a fight with these creatures.

The dim light made it harder to concentrate. The hosts weren't as bulky as anthropoids on Earth. Their fingers were longer, their pelts thinner and of a greenish hue. Lee could see the symbiotic creatures resting right in the middle of each ape's back. He studied them closely. They were slightly more rounded than what he had seen when Haliss stowed away on him, but very similar. He noticed a slight enlargement on one end of the body. It's brain? The tiny cilia or feet barely showed underneath. This one's color appeared lighter than Haliss.

Lee saw a huge monitor in front of him showing a bright sun in the distance. They were flying toward a planet, mostly blue, with a little brown. Suddenly, something plowed into the planet, causing it to explode. The detonation blasted continent-sized chunks into space, leaving nothing but dust and debris. Lee felt great sorrow from the surrounding beings.

Somehow, he understood he had seen Haliss' planet destroyed, and these creatures were now homeless vagabonds. Next, he saw the ship visiting different worlds, studying, exploring, but usually not staying. Some worlds were wet, others dry. Some even had similarities to Earth.

Lee gazed at the monitors and saw other ships behind them.

<Fzillins. Our enemy who has tried to destroy our people, the kreon, for many, many planet revolutions. They destroyed our planet. Now they are trying to annihilate the last of us. They are afraid of us.>

Did you use them for hosts?

<No. They, like you, are too high on the intelligence scale. We didn't even try.>

The ape creatures got older, and some eventually died. There were babies among the apes, but they gradually decreased in numbers. The scenes came faster and faster, like watching a sped-up movie. How long did these kreons live?

<We are long-lived, but not immortal. We pass memories to the young of our people. My sires were younglings when the Fzillins destroyed our planet. I feel the elders' pain from the memories I inherited.>

The kreon explored more planets, but never settled. Some animals they met became hosts, most did not. Finally, the ship landed in Antarctica. Actually, it appeared to be a controlled crash landing. Lee watched through a host's eyes as the kreon ship sped through the atmosphere. Too fast, he thought. The ship made a belly landing, sliding and spewing up snow and ice. Finally, the craft slid to a stop. Lee had to admire the pilot's skill in keeping the spaceship intact.

He watched through a host's eyes. *Your host?*

<Yes.>

The kreon and their hosts found a remote hiding place near their ship, in a lava tube below Mt. Erebus. By now, the hosts were mostly the ape creatures. Any other hosts had already died. Their ship appeared smaller than the first one he had seen, and needed not only repair, but had lost the last of its fuel.

Some kreons became impatient with their old hosts and wanted to find humans to become their new hosts. Lee shuddered, thankful they hadn't landed in Central Park. He continued to watch sped-up memories as a year passed. They worked on their ship using old hands.

I am still not seeing where you and your hosts…

<The denbra.>

I am not seeing where these denbra are getting anything from this relationship.

Suddenly, Lee saw the denbra in their natural habitats, swampy mud pits filled with ferocious reptiles. The reptilian hunters ate many of their young and constantly hunted the denbra. *So, you pulled them out of their habitat and put them on your spaceships because they were in danger.*

<We saved their young from death and disease. We taught them skills and increased their lifespan.>

Lee's aching body told him the debate wasn't worth it. Then he saw the human scientists finding the alien's hidden refuge inside one of the lava tubes of Mt. Erebus. The desire to try humans as hosts came to the forefront of the alien bickering once more. Some kreons wanted to use the newcomers as hosts. Haliss allowed him to feel the other kreon's abhorrence to the idea.

<Until then, our rules firmly stated our hosts had to be no higher than the fifth level on the intelligence scale. Humans are well above. We made no attempt in the year we lived near the volcano to use any humans as hosts.>

There's few humans in Antarctica anyway, Lee thought a little smugly.

Haliss ignored his comment. <I am almost done. When your people discovered us, our leaders came up with a plan to get more hosts.

I am assuming the scientists knew nothing about this plan. At least I gathered as much from Dr. Baker.

<You are correct. One scientist knew Dr. Wilson and had heard about *Sea Dragon*. Now it seemed possible to get new hosts and repair materials and fuel.>

So the scientists contacted Dr. Wilson and enticed us down to Antarctica.

<Yes. Dr. Wilson came eagerly. The promise of a payment for your submarine's services brought the rest of you down. By using such a preeminent scientist as a host or a prisoner, the leadership could get what they needed to fix their spaceship. Then they could leave Earth and outrun their enemies.>

Along with human hosts.

<I am sorry, Captain. When Dr. Wilson came down and my host died, Dr. Baker volunteered to be my host. I realized then humans and kreons were not completely compatible, although Dr. Baker tried very hard. While her sickness interfered with her ability to host me, there were other issues.>

Like what?

<Humans cannot supply all the essentials our people need.>

Are you serious? So, you take more? Is that why I feel so rotten?

<No. I am only taking what I need to stay in existence.>

But we are not compatible!

<That's why we need your help. If we cannot stop them, the leadership will force some of your people to become hosts. Dr. Baker's, as well as my goal, became to warn you. Dr. Wilson realized the danger, too.> Haliss showed a memory, through Dr. Baker's eyes, of Dr. Wilson writing a note, and handing it to her.

Lee heard Doc telling Susan Baker the importance of giving the note to him. Making sure he read it. Lee remembered stuffing the note into his pocket unread.

He came to himself, still shivering. He blinked and gazed at Meyers, whose wide, frightened eyes studied him.

Chapter Thirty-four

"Are you all right, Captain? You scared the hell out of me when you passed out."

"My passenger gave me a history lesson. Let's get out of here. I can explain more later," he muttered. His legs felt like cooked noodles.

"We can send another team out to take care of the dead scientist."

He remembered what Haliss had told him and realized they couldn't send anyone else out here. The doctor's body would have to be left here until they could figure out how to rescue Doc and the other scientists. "You have some aspirin?" The guy with the jackhammer in his head began working harder. Lee bent over, moaning softly, laying his forehead on the cold ground. For some insane reason, it felt good. Meyers' hand lay on his shoulder.

"Yes, sir. If you can wait until we get to the cat."

Lee rose to a sitting position and opened his eyes to the same dimness of the Antarctic vista. Frozen rocks, frozen ground, and frozen air.

"We're in the middle of a hell of a quandary and I'm not a good enough diplomat or strategist to figure our way out." Lee dug the note out of his pocket. With shaking hands, he opened it. It took a few seconds for his eyes to focus. 'Lee, I'm not allowed to leave the alien base, so Susan is bringing Haliss to you. Haliss will need you as a host for a short time and will explain everything.' The last seemed to be written quickly. He stuffed it back in his pocket.

"You were talking about aliens? You saw an alien?" Meyers's eyes looked him over skeptically.

Lee pointed his thumb over his shoulder. "Yes. With Dr. Wilson's assurances the alien is an emissary who doesn't mean us any harm." With Meyers' help, he got to his feet.

<So you understand the problem?>

Sure! You have one of our crewmembers and several other human prisoners. Your leaders want to know if we would make suitable hosts, and if our submarine would supply what you need to repair your ship, including hosts. All we poor bubbleheads have to do is to solve this little Gordian's knot you and those scientists created. He felt Haliss's puzzlement in his mind, but he didn't care. "Let's get back to the cat. We're going to run out of daylight and stamina. Actually, I think I already have." *Oh, and Haliss, when we get back, there will be an executive meeting. I will **not** keep secrets from my crew.* The kreon stayed silent.

The communicator buzzed. Then Henderson called out. "Skipper. Meyers!"

"We're here," Meyers replied.

Lee dug into his pocket for his communicator. The pain in his head eased a bit. "Ensign, we found one scientist near death. She had a message I will deliver at an executive meeting when we're back on the boat. We're going to do the best we can to bury Dr. Baker and then return." He stuffed the communicator back in his pocket.

"I'll get her, Skipper."

"Stack rocks, ice—make a cairn if we can."

"Don't we need to take her body back for an autopsy?"

"We know one of two things killed her. Her cancer or her passenger," Lee pointed out.

<She had a human disease! I did not kill her!>

How do you know? Weren't you here to test the viability of humans hosting you guys?

<I may have had some effect on her, but she had the human disease attacking her body just as she said.>

You get to find out from me just how much might be cancer and how much is the effects of hosting you. She said the cancer worked faster than she thought, Lee replied. *And right now, I feel like hell and I didn't before.*

<This is so new. We have always worked hard to make sure the hosts do not suffer.>

Other than the loss of freedom....

<How can a lower form understand loss of freedom, or having freedom?>

I don't know. I had a dog once that resented staying in the fenced yard. Whenever he could, he escaped to run and play with the other dogs. Lee showed Haliss a mental picture of his dog.

"Captain?"

He jerked his attention back to Meyers. In shock, Lee realized Meyers had partially covered Dr. Baker's body while he commiserated with Haliss. He picked up a couple of stones within a short distance of the cairn and lugged them over to Meyers. After a short time, they finished burying the body.

"We don't have any way to mark the grave," Lee said.

"Let's use this." Meyers tore a five-foot strip from a roll of bandages and anchored one end under a rock. The wind picked up the cloth, and it floated up and down in the freshening breeze.

"I should say something." Lee tried to figure out an appropriate homage. Very little came to his mind since he didn't know her. "Dr. Susan Baker, a dedicated scientist, came and studied a forbidding and dangerous place. She continued her quest even when illness threatened her life. She died trying to help others. May we see a viable end of her efforts—peace, cooperation, and friendship." *Where the hell did I pull those words from*, he wondered?

He sighed, shivered and turned down the hill, digging his flashlight out at the same time. Clouds scudded overhead, darkening the landscape. "Let's go home."

"What about the alien, Captain?"

"What about him?"

<Her. I am a female of my species, as best as you understand it. Dr. Baker mentioned it.>

"You didn't want to go to the *Dragon* because of, uh, the alien," Meyers reminded him.

Lee had been adamant. What changed? He couldn't pinpoint just one thing, but with Doc a prisoner, he had no choice. "I have a hitch-hiking alien, Eric. It's a very intelligent symbiont, but I'm not totally compatible hosting one of these aliens." Then he focused on Haliss. *Female*?

<Yes, are you uncomfortable with my gender?>

Actually, I'm not accustomed to someone hitching a ride on my body and in my mind. Lee questioned why a female alien would be worse than a male alien. He surmised it really wouldn't.

He stumbled. Meyer kept him from falling. "I believe now my passenger isn't here to harm any of us. Call it a gut feeling. But, uh, her leaders seem to think we'd be the perfect hosts, so we have to work together to prevent it from happening. There will be precautions when we get back to the *Dragon*, though."

"Yes, sir."

Haliss, I'm not able to concentrate on the conversation and the trail. I would prefer to continue this talk back on the boat.

<I look forward to it, Captain Zuved.>

Lee. If we're this 'close', you might as well address me by my first name.

<Thank you. Haliss is the less formal way to address me.>

Lee kept his concentration on the slope. Meyer stayed close enough to catch him if he stumbled again. He felt the intense cold. It seeped into every part of his body, sapping even more energy. Putting one foot in front of the other became a struggle.

Bates and Robbins appeared out of the dimness. "You okay, Skipper?" the COB asked.

"Considering everything, yes. I'll explain when we're back on the boat." Then he remembered Haliss' unanswered question. *What about the question I asked? The one about if you could control me or another human. The question you never answered? That's another conversation we need to have.*

<The short answer is I could probably control you to some extent, but humans are highly self-willed and the influence would be limited. A more detailed discussion later would be good.>

Lee had to be satisfied with her answer for the moment. The slope became easier, but Bates stayed close by his side.

Bates helped him aboard and Lee fumed about his waning strength. He knew it had to do with his little passenger, who, at present, kept her thoughts to herself.

Bates made his best time to the boat. Lee started leaning back in the seat and felt a mental squawk from Haliss, so he curled up sideways.

Chapter Thirty-five

Before long, the cat parked near the *Dragon*. Lee roused and climbed down with the rest. He studied the sail sticking out through the sheet of ice and again experienced the hesitation he had when Haliss first latched on to him. Would it really be safe for him to go on board? Baker assured him there were no contagions. With a sigh, he realized he didn't have a great deal of choice.

The XO met them at the portable ladder leading up to the conning tower. "Mace, executive meeting in the wardroom in an hour. Have a master at arms present."

Macon's eyebrows almost blended with his hairline. "Lee?"

"I will explain it all to you before the meeting, but make sure there is a master at arms and he has his weapon."

<I assume this has to do with me?>

Indeed, it does. It also has to do with protocol, Haliss. I am trusting Dr. Wilson's judgement, now trust mine. Haliss didn't respond. Lee pulled off his mittens and unzipped his outer coat as soon as he had climbed down inside the sail.

When they reached the officer's wardroom, the chop assistant met them. "Did you want something to drink, sir?"

Lee nodded. "You still have some of my cacao? I am really in the mood for some."

"Yes, sir. I'll fix you up some right now."

"Thanks. Bring in a selection of warm drinks. There'll be a meeting."

"Aye, aye, sir. How about something to eat?"

"I'm not hungry, but the others may be." Lee pulled off his parka and looked at his watch. Almost midnight. A sailor took his gear to stow away. "Take care of the snow cat at first light," he ordered.

Meyers cleared his throat. "You need something to eat, Skipper. A symbiotic relationship is where the organisms get something from each other. I'm not sure what you're getting, but I know your passenger is benefitting. I want to do a blood test and check you over before the start of the meeting."

Mace glanced from Lee to Meyers and back. "Then I heard correctly on Henderson's line?"

Lee nodded, returning his attention back to Meyers. "Sounds more like a parasitic relationship, if you mean Haliss is leeching nourishment off me. We'll be right back, Mace."

Lee could feel an undercurrent of anger from Haliss, but she said nothing. When they got to the sick bay, Meyers opened a cabinet and pulled out what he needed. "Tell me how you feel."

"Still have the headache, although it's milder, and still have increased fatigue."

"I want you to imbibe, not only liquid refreshment, but food. You now have to provide enough nourishment for yourself and this alien."

"I'll do my best, Eric."

Meyers got his vial of blood. "I'll probably take another sample a bit later. I want to see how anemic you are."

"Anemic?"

Meyers pointed to Lee's fingernails. "Yes, Skipper. Anemic." He drew the blood. "Here, take a couple of ibuprofens for your headache and other aches and pains."

"Thanks," Lee said, taking the tablets with a liberal amount of water.

Haliss still said nothing.

When Lee returned to the wardroom, the chop assistants had already laid out several carafes of coffee, tea, cacao, and hot chocolate. He headed toward the brewed cacao, then hesitated. Suddenly, he felt queasy, just from the smell.

"You want me to pour you a cup, Lee?" Mace asked from behind him.

Haliss, is this any of your doing? I can't even have a cup of brewed cacao? And even the smell turns my stomach.

<You like that noxious concoction in the container right in front of you?>

It's cacao, my go-to favorite warm drink; sometimes even my favorite cold drink. It wakes me up in the mornings and keeps me awake during long nights. Why in the world is it turning my stomach now?

"Lee?" Mace asked again.

<Take a tiny taste and I will analyze it.>

Lee took a cup from Macon and tried to drink some, but before the cup reached his lips, Haliss told him to stop. He didn't think he'd be able to actually drink any of it.

<Evidently there is a something in it deadly to my metabolic make-up.>

Putting it down, Lee sent an evil thought. *Good to know.*

<Not unless you really feel you need to. Besides, didn't you see how repelled you were, too? Perhaps you wouldn't be able to drink it anyway.> She sounded smug.

Perhaps. Lee turned to Macon, who stared at him strangely. "Let's go sit down while we wait." He grabbed a cup of coffee. No hesitation from his stomach on this one. He turned the chair around and sat down. It felt good getting off his feet.

"What's going on, Lee. I didn't hear everything." Macon's hazel eyes gazed at him in worry.

Lee sipped the coffee. While he didn't enjoy coffee as much as most submariners, this tasted good and it certainly warmed him. It felt wonderful going down his throat. "You'll get the entire story in a few minutes when the executive crewmembers get in here, but Doc came down here and stepped right into a hornet's nest. The research scientists who invited him came across an alien outpost. The aliens are symbiotic, using hosts to get around."

"Seriously?"

Lee nodded. "And they apparently have internal issues among themselves, just like Congress. Some of them wanted to use the scientists for hosts because their hosts are dying of old age. The others pointed out it's against their rules to use hosts who are high on the intelligence scale, but the leaders overruled the others."

"Damn!"

"Exactly, but they sent one of the kreon with a volunteer host to meet us."

"Dr. Baker."

"Yes."

"But she died, Lee."

"Indeed, she did, Mace. And I became the next volunteer."

Macon's eyebrows made another northern journey.

"Just help me out with this. A lot of these people won't like what I say."

"Sure, whatever I can do."

Some heads of departments were entering and grabbing a cup of coffee or something else equally hot. The master at arms came in and stood near the skipper. "Grab a cup of coffee and come back and sit down, Benson. You'll understand why Mister Macon invited you to attend shortly."

Bates joined them, a steaming cup in his hand. "Chief, did you make sure the scientists are represented?" Lee asked.

"Yes, sir."

As if on cue, a group of six scientists walked in together. It appeared to him everyone in a leadership role who wasn't on duty showed up. Lee stood. "I wanted to give an update of what's going on and what we found out there. Dr. Wilson didn't come back with us, but there's a good reason." He noticed the curious looks at the Master at Arms. "There is a good reason for Chief Benson, too. All in good time." He took a deep breath.

<Will these humans be as obstinate and emotional as you were?>

Some humans would have squashed you against the rocks by now, but this is a very intelligent and reasonable group. I picked them for this submarine for a reason. Humans are used to acting on their own decisions and impulses. We are not used to having someone sharing our bodies and our minds with us.

<But will they do the same thing you did?> she asked.

Are you worried? No, don't answer. Just let me handle this.

<Very well.>

"Captain?" Macon nudged.

Everyone had been staring at him during the inner conversation, their looks turning to concern.

"Excuse me. I called this meeting to let everyone know just what's going. Doc sent us to a specific rendezvous site to meet Dr. Wilson's representative, Dr. Susan Baker. Unfortunately, she had cancer and died right after we arrived."

One scientist, Dr. Pamela Renning, gasped. "I know, uh, knew her."

"Ensign Meyers buried her the best way he could. Conditions didn't allow us to bring her body back."

"She would have preferred it that way, anyway. She didn't have any family, and she loved her research," Renning added.

Lee nodded. "Now comes the interesting part. Dr. Baker didn't come alone. Apparently, the science team came across a hidden alien refuge in the lava tubes of Mt. Erebus." He waited a few seconds for the various reactions to calm down.

"Aliens? What kind? Are you serious?" were some of the comments Lee heard. There were looks of disbelief, which he understood. Some gasps of fear. There were also a couple of smiles and dreamy looks. He assumed those were the people hoping for E.T. to show up in their closet. "These aliens are a symbiotic race, the superior species making use of hosts in order to get around. They are trying to make repairs on their spaceship so they can leave."

"If I understood you correctly, Captain, these aliens use other creatures as their hosts," one of the other scientists said. "Including humans?"

Chapter Thirty-six

"Normally, no. It's against their species' rules to use higher intelligence creatures for hosts. However, they are losing their regular hosts to old age, so some of them are ready to try us."

"Like hell," Dobbins snapped.

Lee nodded. "That's what I said. Let me continue, Chief." He finished his cup of coffee. A chop assistant picked it up to refill it. "Thanks, Carter."

Now came time for the bombshell. "Part of Dr. Wilson's reason for being here became the means to test whether humans would be suitable hosts. The group of scientists who discovered these aliens believed they only wanted help to fix their spacecraft. Then help to get fuel so they could leave. They wanted Doc's help to accomplish their goals. Apparently, that's what most of the aliens want, too, but their leaders overruled them. For now, Doc is an important hostage so the kreons can get what they need to get off planet, including acquiring hosts. I have no problem considering their request for materials and fuel, but not the host business." He took another breath.

<You are doing very well, Lee.>

Lee snorted. "Dr. Baker acted as a host to one of these kreons. She did it voluntarily. The kreon she hosted had orders to check the viability of using humans as replacements since we are a vastly superior species from their normal hosts. Please remember, that is what they ordered the kreon to do. What she really intends is to work with us to rescue our people and finish the repairs of their ship, so they can leave the planet, so to speak. She and like-minded kreons don't agree with the radical kreon leadership."

Dr. Garcia raised his hand. "Captain, you said Dr. Baker died. She hosted this alien. Where is it now?"

Now came the moment of truth. "The alien's name is Haliss. The friendly kreons need our help to overthrow their leadership. Dr. Wilson sent Haliss to me. I have the kreon symbiont."

The room erupted. Chief Dobbins didn't bother to raise his hand. He just stepped forward, his disfavor on his face, and his gray eyes boring in Lee's. "Captain, may I speak freely?" he shouted over the eruption.

Lee called for quiet and nodded to the weaponry chief.

"You brought an alien aboard? What if we get infected with something or it takes over one of us? Who's saying this thing hasn't already compromised you?"

Lee took a deep breath. "Ensign Meyers can attest to the fact I only wanted to jump off an ice floe when Haliss, um, partnered with me. Your questions reflect what went through my mind."

"What changed your mind? Sir." Dobbins insisted, his arms crossed over his chest.

"First, Dr. Baker assured me tests were done and in the twenty-five days they've been in proximity to the aliens, there is no sign of sickness on either side. As to being compromised, it's always a possibility, but Haliss has been forthcoming. I also received a note from Doc telling me about the situation. I trust Doc."

"But Dr. Wilson could be compromised."

"He could, but I don't think so, Chief. Let me tell you some more and then we'll go from there."

"Is the alien the reason for Billy being here, sir?" Bates asked, pointing to the Master at Arms. "And does it hurt?"

"For the first question, Chief, yes. This submarine and everyone on her are my foremost concern. If I go off the deep end, I want someone around to make sure I don't do something stupid and endanger you and the boat. As to does it hurt, it certainly did at first, now it's mainly a headache and fatigue. I want to reassure you I am pretty convinced of Haliss' true motives, but I will take no chances."

"Could we take it off, Captain?" Mace asked.

"Haliss is just below my shoulder blades. And if necessary, I certainly would want you to. However, right now, I would prefer to learn more and to work with her. We have a dozen people who need rescuing."

"You said you don't feel this alien has compromised you. But could it control you?" Dr. Farr asked.

Lee didn't have an absolute answer to this question. "She could to a certain degree but chooses not to."

"Were you distracted at the beginning of the meeting because of the alien's influence?" Farr asked. His eyes shone with curiosity.

"No. Haliss and I were having a conversation. I haven't learned to communicate internally and externally at the same time. By the way, while I am still coherent, I will continue to serve as your captain, but I will share the command with the XO. Commander Macon will be on equal status as myself. I know it sounds strange, but he just moved up a bit on the chain of command. Consider it having two captains."

"Couldn't that get confusing?" Mace asked.

"I guess it could, but in the long run, it doesn't matter. The crew and scientists can come to you, Mace, especially if I am distracted or too tired to make a rational decision. I will explain more to you after the meeting." He glanced over the group. As Lee expected, some of the crew gazed at him like he had grown another head. In a way, he had. The scientists observed him like some kind of specimen.

<Could you relay something from me?>

Sure. Go ahead. "Wait a minute. Haliss wants to say something."

<My people are an old species and almost extinct. We try to exist without hurting others, which is why we have kept our host laws for so long. Using a human as a host is against my principles, doubly so, since two humans have agreed to let me share their 'personal space.' The kreon, my people, are desperate to escape our enemies, but more desperate to not enslave anyone. I beg you for your help against the three command kreons who want to take humans against their will.>

Lee conveyed the message as closely as he could. It grew quiet in the wardroom when he finished.

Dobbins raised his hand this time. "Ask the alien why they don't just boot their leaders out? Vote them out, force them out, whatever."

<Chief Dobbins asks a good question.>

One I had wondered about but hadn't asked. And the answer is?

<There is something about our internal make-up making it abhorrent to oppose our leaders to the point of overthrowing them. The leadership of three commanders usually works. Because they will compromise and come up with the best decision and outcome for all kreons and their hosts. This situation is unusual and we can't overcome the leadership on

our own. Cultural blocks prevent us. I guarantee if we ignore this threat, the leadership will find some way to use humans. If they can find enough suitable hosts, we will procreate and therefore, need even more hosts.>

Lee winced, but he repeated her answer as close as he could.

The room became even quieter.

"Ask her if she has considered clones or robots," Dr. Garcia asked.

<Robots are out of the question, because we have to take some nourishment from our hosts, but we make sure they are not, themselves, malnourished. As to clones, we have been trying to clone our hosts for some time since they stopped procreating. In theory, this would be the ideal way to solve the host problem. Do humans have such a capability?>

In a very limited capacity. "Haliss said you asked a great question, Doctor. Robots are unfeasible, but the kreon would welcome the ability to create clones and Haliss asked if we could do that. Dr. Garcia, do you know something the rest of us don't know?"

Dr. Garcia shrugged. "I keep up on the updates. It's slow. Some breakthroughs, but relatively few since Dolly, the sheep."

<Sheep?>

See if you can pick up my mental picture.

<I see what you are talking about. Thank you.>

Suddenly, Lee felt falling-down tired. He couldn't think straight, and it became hard to keep his eyes open. "I think we need to meet again at oh seven hundred. Hopefully, we can brainstorm and I'll have talked more extensively with my guest."

Everyone filed out except Meyers, the man at arms Benson, Dr. Garcia, and Mace. Lee was ready to head to his cabin, but Meyers stopped him. "Sir, you don't look too good. I think I need to take another blood sample and see what your numbers are. A cup of hot coffee isn't doing much more than give you a short caffeine rush. I think I am going to order a high test IV."

"What?" Lee stood up, but the room seemed to weave and spin. Mace grabbed him.

"Sick bay, Lee. I think your passenger has stolen your lunch."

<I don't understand what Commander Macon said.>

You are taking my nutrients and things keeping my body going. "Don't feel so hot."

"You look like death warmed over, my friend." Mace wrapped his arm around Lee's shoulder and aided him down the corridor to the tiny sick bay. He pulled down the bunk and helped the captain onto it. Lee remembered nothing after he lay down. He just heard a voice in his head. <I must report. I must let the leadership think . . . they… are … win…ning.>

Chapter Thirty-seven

Mace watched the Ensign take a blood sample and run it in a small machine set up in the corner. In all his time at sea, he could not have imagined something like this. Lee looked like hell and he wondered if they would have to remove the creature.

Garcia studied his patient's fingers. "I believe the captain is anemic."

"He is. I am going to start a basic IV and I might ask for a transfusion before the night is over."

"We're the same blood type," Mace said.

Meyers shook his head. "You are in charge when the skipper isn't. I don't need both of you under the weather. I'm going to give him a B12 shot, the IV, and when he wakes up, a decent meal—at least something he can tolerate until later. Hopefully, those three things will take care of both of our patients' needs for the moment." He reached for a cabinet and found Garcia in the way. "I think the captain's going to be fine, Doctor. Why don't you go get some shut-eye, too?"

Mace continued to look Lee over as Garcia left. "What does the alien look like? It must be small."

"I think it is," Meyers replied. "I haven't seen her. Perhaps now is the time to find out." He unbuttoned the skipper's shirt and partly eased it off Lee's torso. Then Meyers rolled him onto his stomach. In the middle of the captain's back lay a small, smartphone-sized hunk of liver-colored flesh, with what appeared to be tiny hairs underneath. But it looked very much attached. "Holy Mother of God."

"Ditto," Macon breathed.

Meyers replaced the shirt, not buttoning it back.

Mace started unfolding a chair. Meyers stopped him. "Sorry, sir, but you need to get some sleep, too. I don't think you're on duty right now."

"No."

"I'm going to take a nap and let Benson watch the skipper, but you get some sleep in your own rack."

"Let me know if anything changes."

"I will, Commander."

Chapter Thirty-eight

Something propelled Lee through the water. His arms guided him toward faint lights in the distance. Then he noticed the absence of scuba gear. How could this be possible? How could he breathe underwater? He swam toward the brightest light, again wondering why he could breathe underwater. Then he realized his body was almost transparent. He existed in this place, but he didn't. He traveled with someone—Haliss! But not as a fist-sized piece of liver. Her body or presence resembled some kind of geometric shape of swirling color. Several other avatars, all geometrically shaped but with different colors, traveled with them.

<Commander Haliss. You have been among the humans. What is your report?>

<They are difficult, but I think we can overcome the problem with time. I told them the truth about crash-landing and needing help to fix our spaceship. Like these others, they seemed eager to help. Unfortunately, the scientist hosting me died before we reached their vessel. I am using the commander of the submarine as a host. He believes he's contacted a totally benign alien race. Their vessel has distinct possibilities to use for our ship's repair.>

The largest shape seemed to brighten. <Then we need to guide them here. Let them think they can affect a successful first contact. Bring them here!>

<This vessel is a submarine, an underwater vessel. It cannot go on land and we are some distance away.>

The leader spoke again. <Then perhaps we should rendezvous with them to the north of our base. Separate them from their ship and when they are subdued, we can board it.>

<What about the ones you have as prisoner now?>

<We have not taken them as hosts yet. They are still under the delusion they are privileged to be the first to meet an alien race. They are working very hard to help us find a solution to getting into space again,> the leader answered.

<Your report is acceptable,> one of the other avatars said. <We will use the human communications to arrange a place for the vessel to come close enough for a rendezvous.>

As Lee swirled back through the dimness, he felt anger and betrayal. While he watched and listened, he wondered why he hadn't reacted to this betrayal. He wondered if Haliss even realized he came with her. Then he remembered the last thing she said to him. Could Haliss have been dissembling?

His stomach rumbled and his head still hammered away, although it had changed to a ball-peen hammer rather than a jackhammer. When he opened his eyes, he saw Meyers dozing in a chair. There was no sign of the master at arms. Out in the corridor, most likely. Despite the sick headache, Lee craved a nice, large glass of water. His throat felt as dry as Death Valley. He slowly sat up.

Chapter Thirty-nine

"Skipper! You're awake. How are you feeling?"

Lee knew better than to hold back from their chief medical officer. While not a full-fledged medical doctor, Meyers was a very capable nurse practitioner. In a pinch, Lee had seen their CMO do minor surgery. They were lucky to have him. "Still have the headache, but not as bad as before." A blanket draped around his shoulders. "I'm feeling a little less like a popsicle and more like a human being. Still worn out, but not as bad."

"Any nausea?"

He shook his head. "No, I'm ravenous."

Meyers grinned. "Great. I'll have Cookie send some comfort food. Cacao? I noticed you backed off from it at the meeting."

Lee sighed. "No, I'll take coffee. Cacao is not an option."

<Lee?>

Did you have to take me along when you reported to your superiors?

<No, I didn't have to, but I hoped you had heard enough before you went into your rest stage to figure out everything going on. I wanted you to hear what the leaders said.>

At first, I was mighty pissed, but then I remember you telling me something before I passed out. And no, I didn't go into a rest phase. My body shut down. I suspect Ensign Meyers gave me some pick-me-up stuff after I went into la-la land.

Lee looked at the place on his arm where a Band-Aid now rested. "Eric, is this from an IV?"

"Yes, it is. You were dehydrated. I also gave you a B-12 shot, but I think a hearty breakfast will do as much or more."

"Thanks, Eric. And don't mind if I act distracted. Seems I need to conference with my guest."

"Go for it, but when breakfast comes, you eat it while it's still hot."

"Gladly."

<When you were 'passed out' I couldn't see, but I heard a little. You have a very loyal group of comrades.>

We have only been together for about six months. We are a hand-picked crew.

<Including you?>

All of us. Doctor Wilson and another man, Admiral Drumwright, made the first selections, then each leader chose those who would be under him. The admiral watched the Dragon *launched and died a short time later. Sea Dragon is his legacy.* Lee felt a bit of sadness.

<We once had those kinds of leaders. Unfortunately, the Leadership of Three doesn't seem able to…lead.>

So what you told the other kreon—one of your leadership—I assume you're were trying to buy time?

<What does this buy time mean? Do you mean to stall for time?>

Yes.

<I thought if you had to take your submarine to a different meeting place, there would be time to figure out a way to overcome the Leadership of Three.>

Tall orders for people who really don't want to get involved in the middle of alien warfare, especially internal wrangling. We have enough of our own.

<When your people found us, they included themselves. If, for no other reason than for the Leadership to consider humans as the ultimate hosts. If they can force you to serve as hosts, we will stay, procreate, and build up defenses against our enemies. And yes, we know about some of your human squabbles.>

Then you know there would be a great deal of rebellion for your leadership to quell. Our history is full of examples of humans fighting for the right to be free. Aren't your people searching for some place to live in peace—to be free?

<We are a people trying to survive.>

"Here it is, Skipper," Meyers announced.

Lee appreciated the timing of this interruption. Things were getting way too serious. The young chop assistant carried a tray piled high with food. "Holy cow! Everything smells and looks phenomenal. Thanks, Taryn." He noticed the large mug of coffee, freshly made.

"You're welcome, sir. I'll come back and get the tray later."

Lee glanced at his watch. Oh five hundred. *Let me eat in peace, Haliss. Then we will both be better off to scheme and plot against the Death Eaters.*

<Death Eaters?>

A reference to the bad guys in a popular human entertainment. He showed her a better visual. *Humans have very active imaginations.*

<Obviously.>

Lee felt a kind of sadness drifting through his mind. *Haliss, it's too bad our peoples have to deal with this mess. I wish we could solve our problems so we could exchange ideas as equals, not host and controller.*

<As do I. Eat your breakfast before Ensign Meyers has to remind you. We can discuss more after you have finished.>

You just want some, too. Lee turned his attention to the tray. Despite being made from powder, the eggs were just right with butter, cheese, salt, and pepper adding flavor. The plates on the tray held grits, bacon, fluffy biscuits, and S.O.S. of just the right consistency. "Wow! Grab a fork, Eric. There is no way in hell I can eat all of this."

"Eat all you can, Skipper. You know you're eating for two."

Lee almost dropped his fork in surprise, then he laughed. "One freebie is all you get. I'll hear it again, but no more from you."

"Aye, aye, sir." Meyers laughed. He waited until the skipper finished and then he ate the rest. "You're right, this is great. By the way, I checked on your passenger. She looks like a rectangular piece of liver."

<If you want anyone else to enter these conversations, all they need to do is touch me.>

Meyers put the empty tray on the chair.

"Go ahead. Touch her."

"Huh? Seriously?"

"She would like to communicate with you. It might be easier if I don't have to pass along messages. You can make your own assessments." Lee pulled off his shirt and Haliss climbed up to the top of his tee shirt. It tickled this time. A far cry from when she first latched on.

Meyers reached around and let his finger hover over Haliss. Then he gingerly touched the alien.

Chapter Forty

<Greetings, Ensign Meyers. My compliments on the very competent care you have given your commanding officer.>

Meyers's eyes grew large, and he jerked his hand back. "I could hear a voice in my head."

"Meet Haliss."

He touched her again. "Glad to meet you, Ms. Haliss."

<You can think your comments or questions if you want to, Ensign.>

The three of them had a brief conversation before Meyers pulled back. "Incredible!"

As if on cue, Mace strode into the cubby. "You look a lot better than you did last night, even if you are underdressed."

"I feel a heckuva lot better, too. And the underdressed is so Ensign Meyers could talk to Haliss."

"Seriously? Anyone can speak to your passenger?"

"Meet our friend. Just touch her and you'll be able to hear her. Then you'll understand a little better what's going on."

Mace did so, and his mouth dropped open.

<I am glad you will help me throw the Leadership of Three out on their ear and clean up the pigpen.>

Mace and Lee laughed.

You picked up those phrases from my unfiltered thoughts? Hopefully, nothing dirty.

<Dirty? As in unclean?>

No, as in doing something inappropriate, in a sexual nature. Uh, kreons have sex?

<Yes, we do, Lee. Our hosts, in the past, have as well. I understand what you were alluding to.> Slight humor permeated her thoughts.

Mace pulled back from the unusual conversation.

Haliss resumed her position between Lee's shoulder blades. He grunted as she made the previous connection. Some pain, but nothing horrible. He grew serious. "After I've cleaned up and changed, we need another executive meeting. Just a few of us."

"You learned something?"

"No solutions, but I learned a few facts to commiserate over. You on duty?"

"No, just got off and heading to chow."

"When you're done, come to my cabin. The three of us need to have a bit of discussion before we meet with a bigger group."

"Sure, Lee. I'll snag me a cup of joe and some toast."

He shook his head. "Have a decent breakfast. We can wait that long. The biscuits and S.O.S. are delicious this morning."

Macon nodded. "I will. I won't be long, though."

"You think the master at arms can help you get to your quarters all right, Captain?" Meyers asked.

"Yes."

"I'll wait outside your door," Hentley, Benson's replacement, said when they arrived at his cabin.

"Thanks, Chief."

Once inside, Lee unbuttoned and pulled off his ship suit, then hung it on the edge of his rack. He still felt like he needed a nap. Maybe later, when they figured out a game plan. Right now, he only used disposable cleansing towels to spit bathe, then he pulled on clean underwear. He turned his backside to the mirror to view Haliss laying serenely on his back. She had been quiet. "Next time it won't be cleansing towels. It'll be a shower. You good for a dunking?"

<Moisture doesn't bother me. I am very glad you are feeling better.>

And you?

<I think the food you call breakfast aided both of us.>

Maybe we can get somewhere deciding what to do with the Leadership of Three. I doubt they will take long before issuing orders.

<I agree.>

He pulled on a clean outfit.

Someone knocked on his door. "Lee?"

"Come on in." He started buttoning his shirt but thought better of it. Haliss might need to discuss something with Mace, too.

The executive officer entered. "How are you doing?"

"Still got a slight headache, still tired, but otherwise, okay."

"We got a communication from Haliss' people a few minutes ago."

"Where do they want us to go?"

"The coordinates are seventy degrees south and 160 degrees east. Place called Oates Land. Near the bottom of Victoria Land."

"You look it up?"

"Sure did. Won't take us too long to get there. What are we going to do then?"

"Don't know yet. Contact Haliss. I think this needs to be a three-way conversation."

Mace lightly touched the kreon. "What do you think they'll do when we reach your base, Haliss?"

<Probably subdue your delegation and take you over. Most of the hosts are nearing the end of their life cycles and stamina. They are tired and only want to rest.>

"I would imagine we can't take weapons in there. They'll detect those immediately," Lee said.

"Too bad we can't smuggle some kind of gas," Macon suggested. *Sleep gas or something similar.*

<Such a gas would be a simple solution, but they would detect anything foreign before you walked into the base.>

Lee frowned. "I feel like I'm missing something."

Macon watched him. Someone knocked on the door.

"Enter," he called out. One of the Chop assistants came in with two cups and a small pot. It smelled like coffee.

The orderly put the tray on the pull-down desk and left. Mace poured fresh coffee into a cup and added a little sugar, handing it to Lee. "I asked them to bring this in. I figured we'd be commiserating for a while." He poured himself a cup, adding plenty of cream and sugar.

Lee looked into his cup. "Oh, but for a cup of cacao. Great stuff. You don't know what you're missing. Either of you."

<Yes, I do. I don't understand how you can enjoy such a noxious substance.>

Lee took another sip of his coffee, and then he almost choked. "We have something! Why the hell didn't I think of it sooner?"

Mace stared at him. "What?"

"Cacao!"

"What? Holy cow, you're right. You weren't even able to taste any because of its toxicity to Haliss. But we can't go in there with a pot of brewed cacao."

"This calls for a conference." Lee motioned for Macon to touch Haliss. *Hallis, can you think of any way to figure out the poisonous ingredient in cacao?*

<No, remember, you couldn't even take a taste. All I know is something in the drink you liked is deadly to me. Or at least would make me very sick.>

Dr. Garcia could not figure it out. Not in the short time we have. The scientists can study this and make some deductions. Otherwise, how much cacao do you think it would take to incapacitate one of your Leadership of Three?

<I doubt it would take very much, considering how abhorrent it is to me just being close to it.>

Lee grabbed the communicator hanging by his door. "Sparks? This is the captain. Find Dr. Garcia and send him to my cabin."

Ten minutes later, Garcia showed up and Lee outlined what he and Macon had discussed. The scientist began tapping information into his iPad.

Chapter Forty-one

"It's not the water, so that leaves the ingredients from the cacao beans, since it's simply brewed cacao powder," Garcia began.

"No caffeine," Lee ventured.

"May I converse with Haliss?" Garcia asked.

Lee sat down backward on the desk chair, allowing the scientist the means to touch her.

<I believe the captain is correct. Whatever ingredient in the cacao toxic to kreons is powerful even in a small quantity.>

"We have no way to test such a theory, even though I can guess it's probably the theobromine. It is a unique ingredient," Garcia offered, glancing at his computer.

<Could this theobromine be ingested by those meeting my people?>

Garcia shook his head. "We have no way to separate the components of the cacao powder."

"We'll need four volunteers to drink the cacao before we meet the Leadership of Three. Perhaps a capsule of finely ground cacao to swallow just before getting there."

"The capsule might be hard to take," Garcia said.

"Just think of it as extra fine dark chocolate," Lee said.

***

Sea Dragon sat just off the ice shelf, not too far from land a day later. From what Lee understood, ships had to stay miles offshore in the past. Probably the effects of global warming. He surveyed the coast, seeing a small station in the distance. One building put out steam or smoke. According to the communications, this was the rendezvous place. Three people, plus himself, would go: Petty Officer Hentley, Chief Bates, and Dr. Sara Benning. She turned out to be a cacao drinker, too. They had their cup of cacao, and each had a capsule to stick in their mouths when they got closer.

Lee enjoyed several quick naps during *Sea Dragon's* trip to this rendezvous, so he felt ready. Ensign Meyers stashed several energy bars in Lee's pocket. His symbiosis with Haliss had to be the only thing keeping him from becoming Porky Pig, he figured.

<Not possible. Your metabolism and mine would not let you get big enough to resemble this rotund animal you pictured in your mind.>

A human exaggeration, he explained.

<When this is over, I hope you will explain several confusing things about your species.>

Perhaps we will have time, especially since your spacecraft will need to be fixed.

<Our long range reconnaissance scout ship crashed here. We have a hidden intergalactic vehicle on one of your outer planetary moons.>

You didn't tell me! Although Lee seemed to remember the ships were different when she gave him kreon history.

<You didn't ask. Neither of us told the other much about their culture at the beginning. Our scout ship needs enough

repairs to get us into space, but now we mostly need fuel. The ship is useless without replenishing the fuel cell.>

What kind of fuel?

<We can adapt what you use in your vehicle.>

Nuclear fuel? No, you can't. If you take our fuel, Sea Dragon is dead in the water, and we don't have the means to get it replaced. Extremely expensive.

<Perhaps we can negotiate something after this crisis ends.>

Perhaps. Lee didn't want to contemplate this monkey wrench in an already complicated scenario.

<You will not be ill-used by us for helping.>

Lee and the others donned their coats. They climbed through the hatch and into the zodiac ferrying them the short distance to the shoreline. Lee climbed out and into the frozen desert. Clouds scudded across the landscape. A gust of wind blew him back into Bates, who staggered but didn't fall.

"I think we need to rope ourselves together, Skipper," Bates suggested.

"I agree, Chief."

With the ropes around their waists, they found it easier to stay upright. The wind didn't ease up, but the group kept up a good pace—one Lee hoped he could maintain. The headache had calmed down in the past day, but the brightness of the sun notched it back up. Still, they made good time and before they had walked an hour and a half; they were approaching the outpost. The building stood in stark contrast to its surroundings, a warehouse-type building several times the size of a three-car garage.

Lee looked back and saw Bates nodding everybody's readiness. Then he reached for the door handle. When he opened the door, he noticed five denbra, wrapped in blankets, standing in front of them.

He held out his hand. "I am Captain Lee Zuved. We are here at your invitation. We would like—" All hell broke loose. The motley apes leaped for his three companions, knocking him aside.

<They didn't waste any time!>

Good. If they had, the cacao might have worn off…. Before he could say anything else, Lee felt two creatures grab his arms, pinning them to his side. Something exploded in his head, and he fell in shock and pain. The creatures held him to the ground, grabbing at his parka. They were trying to get Haliss! He rolled to his side and kicked as hard as he could. One creature fell back, holding an upper limb to its chest.

He kicked again. This host, or its kreon, had figured out his abilities and grabbed his foot. When he fell, Lee felt something hard and metallic under his hand and grabbed it. He swung and hit the alien on the head. It croaked and fell limp on the floor. It still held his leg as it made moaning sounds. Lee kicked again, and the creature rolled away. He staggered to his feet. *Haliss? Haliss, are you there?*

Lee felt a bit of stirring, but nothing more. His head throbbed. Someone screamed. The apes backed off, looking lost and confused.

He stumbled toward his crew. "Chief! Doctor! Hentley!"

Hentley lay on the ground. Lee reached for him and almost got his good arm yanked out. "Hey, it's me, your captain."

Hentley blinked once and then blinked again. "Skipper. Sorry. But the pain."

"Any other thoughts in your head other than your own?"

He slowly shook his head. "There were some before, but they're gone. Now I just have a hell of a headache."

<Pull off the kreon,> Haliss said weakly.

Won't it kill both parties? You told me it would.

<Not when the kreon is near death. A dead kreon can kill the host, too.> She was reviving.

Lee did as directed, reaching under Hentley's parka and shirt, finding the liver-like creature. When he yanked it off and pulled it away, the color had changed to a sickly gray and it appeared sponge-like. He tossed it to one corner. He left Hentley to finish recovering on his own and bent down to help Bates. The chief of boat sat up and snarled at him. "Chief. Chief Bates! It's Zuved, your captain."

"You … did … this!!!" Bates tried to take a swipe at him with his fist, but Lee ducked. "I'll kill you … and the traitor, Haliss…." Bates slowly rose from the floor, weaving as though drunk.

Can I do the same thing, Haliss? Take off the kreon?

<You have little choice.>

"Yes, I do. He's my friend as much as he's my chief of boat."

Lee hooked his leg behind Bates's ankle, knocking him to the ground. Then the captain kneeled on his back. Bates bucked him off. Pain shot up his back when he rolled on the ground. He gasped and tried to get to his feet.

Bates' fist caught him on the shoulder. Lee ducked out of the way of the next swing. Bates continued staggering toward him. The captain kicked, and this time flattened him to the ground. Again, he reached for his COB's back and found the kreon. "Bates, hang on!" He pulled. The chief screamed and then lay still.

Benning slowly rose to her knees.

"Hold still, Doctor," Lee ordered.

"Yes, sir," she panted.

At least Benning had more control of herself. He reached under her parka, her shirt, and her bra and found the squishy mass. Then he pulled it off. Lee tossed it on top of the other dead kreons.

"Thanks, Captain," she gasped. "It hurt like hell, but I think I hurt it more."

He checked Bates, who hadn't moved. "Chief."

Lee heard a soft moan.

"Chief Bates. Come back to us. Chief!" More moaning. "Come on, Terrill. Your wife will kill me if I don't bring you back to the boat alive!"

"I'd … have to feel better … to die."

Lee breathed a sigh of relief and helped the COB up.

Bates held his head in his hands. "Jeez, did it hurt this bad when you got Haliss?"

"At first it hurt like hell." Lee turned his attention to Haliss. *Okay, what about these others?*

<Please approach them.>

He hesitated. Suddenly he blinked and saw his hand touching a kreon laying on its host's arm.

<I'm sorry, Lee. This needed to be done quickly. I had to communicate with the others. To make sure they were still adamant about not using your people as hosts.>

"Checking on the political climate," he muttered, still touching the kreon.

<And I had to make sure your people are safe. What they used to subdue us weakened me somewhat.>

And me. They pack a powerful punch. And are the others safe?

<They are.> Lee heard a different mental voice; one with a distinct quality, deeper? <I am Qi rill, the mind scribe of the Leadership of Three. We would like to have a meeting between our people. I am sorry for the harm done to you and your companions. We were under orders from the Leadership of Three. They are no more. Our loyalties are to the complete group.>

Lee noticed the three kreon-less hosts huddled in a corner. *What will happen to them?*

<There are kreon citizens with hosts who are barely functioning, like the host you killed. These will serve as hosts.> Qi rill paused. <It is all they know.>

Still, they are like slaves.

<I see the picture in your mind and no, they are not the same. These are low on the intelligence scale.>

We're finding out apes on Earth are smarter than most people thought, Lee pointed out.

<We are very thorough in our testing. Which is why so many of our people balked when the Leadership of Three suggested using your race.>

He pointed out Haliss's ease of controlling him.

<No, Lee,> Haliss said. <I exerted great effort, and only for a moment. Maintaining complete control, which is what we need during space flight, would be too difficult. And especially if the host resents the kreon's influence.>

That would happen in the long run with humans. Lee pulled away, and no one argued the point.

The humans and the denbra worked together to make the quarters decently warm as well as clean it up for the incoming humans.

When they finished, Lee asked questions and Haliss allowed him to see some more of their history. He did the same for most of her questions.

Now we need to figure out how to get what you need for your space journey.

<Why wouldn't those who have ownership of the fuels and supplies want to help us?>

Lee laughed. *People and governments seeking exclusive rights to engage with aliens from a distant solar system might delay the supplies. And then there would be those who are more like your*

Leadership of Three and feel they need to destroy all of you for the common good of humanity.

<Really?>

You said you monitored some of our communications. You mentioned to me our paranoia and warlike tendencies. Don't you see that could be possible? We will have to wait and see what kind of magic Dr. Wilson can do among his colleagues.

Lee yawned. The brawl had worn him out. Despite the activity in the small building, he fell asleep sitting backward in the hard metal chair.

Chapter Forty-two

"Lee." Someone gently shook his shoulder. He recognized the voice. "Lee?"

Doc! With a jolt, the skipper woke up, his gaze fixed on Doc Wilson. "You're alright?" Lee studied his colleague, seeing no obvious injuries.

Doc pulled an empty chair near his. "Yes. I'm alright. How are you?"

"Eternally tired, but I can't complain. We accomplished our mission."

"Brilliantly, too. I can't believe I fell for the Leadership's subterfuge. While we're helping them, they're plotting to use us as hosts!"

"Don't beat yourself up, Doc. It's not every day we get to work with an alien race." His head thumped a slow cadence. He dug in his pocket and swallowed three ibuprofens, washing them down with a swallow of water. *Sorry, Haliss.*

<Don't worry about it. Those medicines of yours do not harm me. In fact, I feel a little better after you take them, too.>

"I thought it was strange when they isolated us and then ignored us," Doc said. "So, you're holding up okay?"

He nodded. "Haliss is a considerate passenger. It took some adjusting. Still does. I feel about thirty years older."

"Well, after you're fully awake, we'll do one of those avatar chats."

"I'm awake. You know about those?"

"Yes, I saw one when Haliss and Mjir summoned the rest of us here. It's their version of a computer, the best I can figure out. They said it's the only way so many of their people and ours could take part in this conference. And they want us involved."

"I would imagine, since we have what they need to fire up their scout ship and their intergalactic ship."

Doc's jaw dropped. "They have two spaceships?"

Lee nodded. "They came looking for fuel and their scout ship crash-landed. The Leadership of Three had thoughts of conquest early on."

Doc stood up. "Actually, they had minimal damage to their ship, and have been able to fully repair it in the year they've been here. They're only limited by the ability of their hosts."

Lee pulled himself out of the chair, feeling his joints creak and pop. Doc watched him. Bates stepped up beside him, also watching. He frowned at both men. "I don't look that bad."

Bates grinned. "Do you want me to be honest, sir?"

"No." Lee stretched and then Doc pointed to a table nearby.

Haliss directed him to stand at a certain place near the table. <Stare at a spot on the table just in front of you. Fixate on it. Let nothing distract you.>

Lee did as directed and felt his eyes almost crossing. Suddenly, he saw the same avatar thing he had seen before, and he concentrated on it. Freezing cold crawled from his fingertips, up his arms, and through his body. He couldn't shiver, couldn't wrap his arms around himself, couldn't fasten his parka. Cold, dry ice cold….

He noticed the ship the kreon had been working on. It appeared old, but from a submariner's eye, serviceable. *Nice job,* he thought.

<Thank you,> a voice sounded in his head. It wasn't Haliss.

<I am Kreliss. I am the oldest now. The former Leadership of Three made a wrong conclusion. Even if we become extinct because our hosts die, we cannot go against the laws set up many generations ago. Perhaps it would be a good thing for us to become extinct.>

There were mutterings and undercurrents of other voices, all indistinct.

No, it wouldn't, Lee thought, suddenly realizing the viability of his statement. *Despite how you have evolved, you are intelligent beings. No intelligent being should face extinction.*

No creature deserves extinction. Another voice came into his head. Doc. *What we have to do is figure out a way for kreons to continue their journey, not only into space but also into their own future. Evolution—mutation of the species.*

<How would you propose for us to do such a thing, Doctor?> Kreliss asked. <The ideal would be if we could grow a means of mobility, which is unlikely. The next ideal would be to create some kind of android to host us.>

We have AI, but they are computers and simple robots, Lee offered.

We have worked on the science of clones, but technically it's the same as using a person as a host, Dr. Garcia said. *Or would it?*

<What do you propose?> Kreliss asked.

I don't really know, but if someone created clones to work with your people, then it wouldn't be like you were 'taking' creatures for your use. I know it sounds like the same thing. There's a difference between acquiring a self-sufficient being and constructing one specifically for your needs.

Kind of like taking a puppy and raising it to be a Seeing-Eye dog? Lee asked.

I guess, Garcia said, *that's about the closest analogy I can think of.*

<You said your people have experimented with clones> Haliss interjected. <An animal called a sheep?>

There have been experiments with people. A few clones of people. I know a scientist who has done some experiments. I believe he would share his notes. Garcia paused. *And then I would like to volunteer to be a host. I would like to go with you and help you solve this problem.* His voice softened. *I want to see space.*

<Are you sure? Your captain seems to have physiological issues with hosting.> Kreliss pointed out.

He's being kind, Garcia. Sometimes it hurts like hell and most of the time I am bone tired.

Garcia felt deflated. *Yes, it would make it difficult.*

Are you sure you want to go, Miguel? Doc Wilson asked.

Yes.

Lee had a thought. *Would it be possible, Kreliss, for you to take a resident scientist to help your people solve this problem? No hosting. Would you have room?*

Kreliss responded, <If we can get the fuel we need. But when we came our ship was crowded.>

You lost three of your members and I heard you lost a host, Doc pointed out.

<Three hosts. Two belonging to the Leadership of Three died before they received another kreon,> Kreliss said.

Lee felt a stirring in his mind and wondered about Haliss.

<I want to stay on Earth when you leave, Kreliss,> she ventured. <And yes, I know I can't have a human host. While

we were traveling here on Lee's submarine, I heard songs. They were the songs of some other creature. I heard this while Lee recovered from hosting me and slept. I would like to find out more about this musical creature.>

Lee kept his thoughts to himself, preferring to speak to her in private.

<I do not think it would be wise, Leader Haliss, but it is a matter to discuss later. The more pressing problem right now is fuel. If we can't get fuel, it doesn't matter what any of the participants want to do,> Kreliss stated. His avatar swirled like a tornado, in colors of red, white, and gold.

I can't promise anything, because nuclear fuel is highly regulated, but I will try to find nuclear fuel pellets for you to take on your ship, Doc said. *When will you finish your repairs?*

<We are almost done. Tests are last.>

Of course. To get the fuel, we will need to travel to the places producing the nuclear pellets. I need to discuss with your fuel experts exactly how much you need and how you will store them.

<We will meet again after the rest period,> Kreliss said.

Lee watched the swirling threads of Haliss' avatar dance for a moment, and then he backed away. He felt someone by his side, someone extremely warm, helping to dispel the cold in the room. He began shivering again and pulled his parka tighter around his body.

Then the black tendrils closed on him again and the little guy with the hammer tapped on the inside of his skull.

"Skipper!" Meyers called out close to him. The blackness closed fully.

Chapter Forty-three

Lee woke up on a cot. Mace sat nearby, nursing a cup of steaming coffee. Carefully, he sat up, feeling his joints creak. "Jeez, I feel old."

"That, too, will pass," Macon said. "Got some of your new drink of choice. Fresh and hot." He handed him a steaming cup.

"Thanks." Taking a sip, Lee admitted it tasted and felt very good going down. "All I do is sleep! How long this time?"

"About four hours."

He drank more of his coffee. "My compliments to the chef." Suddenly, Lee heard the creaking, drawn out song of a whale.

<Do you recognize this?>

Yes, it's a whale. Probably a right whale, or a blue or humpback. Lots of whales come down here for the krill in the Antarctic waters.

<Krill?>

Little shrimp-like creatures that baleen whales and other sea mammals eat. This is the song you've been hearing?

<Yes.>

How can you hear it so far away?

<They are powerful. Not loud, but powerful.>

They're loud, too. Our sonar operators hear them inside the boat when they are near.

"Come and get it," Mace cut into his and Haliss' conversation.

Lee walked over to the table laid out with sandwich fixings. After he finished stacking a sub roll, Lee added chips to his plate. He sat down with a group of scientists.

"Holy cow, Lee, that's a more glorious sandwich than the one you did when we graduated from the rank of plebes," Macon teased as he sat down next to him. "Glad you're feeling better."

"You're just jealous. And thanks. By the way, where's Doc?"

"Conferencing with the kreon big wigs," Mace told him.

"Has he said when he wants to leave for his fuel run?"

"Soon, but I haven't heard a definite."

As soon as Lee finished his sandwich, various scientists peppered him with questions. One of the chop assistants brought a plate of cookies.

***

The next day, Lee and the rest of the crew, minus several scientists, headed back to *Dragon*. Haliss had been quiet. An old denbra followed them, bundled up against the elements. Its eyes were downcast, its breath a soft wheezing. The creature didn't appear to have much life left in it.

Lee assumed the hand off would be when they said goodbye at the boat. He wondered why they hadn't separated at the base station. Haliss didn't say, and he didn't ask. She told him Kreliss wanted her to return to the galactic ship when she exchanged hosts.

The sun shone brightly, but the wind stripped it of any advantage. Still, this hike beat the first one to Mt. Erebus. Lee felt a touch of sadness and wondered if it came from Haliss and affecting him or the other way around. He had actually become used to having a companion. Even as short a time as a few days. This had been a real learning curve.

It took them half of the morning to reach the sub. Harris supervised the loading of the cat with supplies for the scientists staying behind and the hosts.

Lee stood watching the activity near the gangplank. *I am going to miss you, Haliss. Despite the side-effects and the rough beginning, it has been interesting.*

<I will miss you, Lee. Seeing your world through your eyes has been a wonderful experience for me.> She paused a moment. <It's been enlightening. I have learned… I do not feel the same way I did before.>

You have taught me a lot.

<And you, me.>

I would imagine you will take off as soon as we get you the fuel. Lee felt rustling under his shirt. Presumably getting ready to swap hosts. He braced for their separation.

<I need to leave soon. Hopefully, the parting will not be as painful for you as the beginning of our partnership. I am releasing now.>

Her cilia moved in place on his back and then a sharp pain shot through his body. Not as bad as before.

"Skipper!" Bates called out.

Lee felt Haliss sliding down his sleeve. Momentary dizziness kept him bent over, but soon he straightened up. Bates stayed close to his side. The ape creature moaned and stepped from one foot to the other. The lost look in its eyes seemed deeper. Before anyone could say anything, it dashed to the edge of the ice and jumped in.

"What happened?" Lee asked, totally confused.

"I guess she committed suicide," Bates replied. "She slid from under your parka and then slipped right into the drink."

"Huh? The ocean?"

"Same place the ape went," Bates scratched his chin. "Do you want me to contact the aliens?"

"Yes, Chief, please. Let them know what happened." He stared at the spot where the denbra, and before it, Haliss, had slid into the ocean. She had defied her orders. And followed her dream. He hoped she found her whale.

"Aye, aye, sir."

The others returned to their duties. Lee, still feeling off, followed Bates on board. Then he realized that while he hated the intrusiveness of having another entity share his mind, now he felt very alone. Mace met him in the control room. "I heard Haliss went into the ocean,"

"Yes, and her host followed."

"I'm really sorry." Mace said, his voice soft. "She turned out to be a very interesting…person."

"She told me she had found a whale willing to host. I suspect the denbra has earned the freedom death brings."

"Really? How would she get to a whale?"

Lee shrugged. "I don't know, but she seemed confident it would work out."

"By the way, Ensign Meyers wants you in sick bay. Then hit the rack. There isn't a blessed thing you can do right now."

Meyers drew another blood sample. Before he finished, Lee received a summons from the communications officer. He grabbed the mike. "Zuved here. Kind of busy in sick bay now."

"When you're finished, Captain, the kreons want to talk to you."

"I'll be up in a few minutes."

Meyers did the blood test, then announced, "Well, the good news is your red count numbers are up. I think they were probably going up before Haliss left, but I am going to put you on vitamins for a couple of weeks to build up your iron."

Lee buttoned his shirt and headed forward.

"Okay, Sparks, what's up?" he asked when he returned to the control room.

"They are standing by." 'Sparks' made the call and handed Lee a headset.

"To whom am I speaking?" Lee asked.

"Dr. Garcia, Captain. I'm the go-between."

"Go ahead, Miguel."

"Doc's on his way back to the *Dragon*."

"Figured he would be."

"And Kreliss wanted to let you know Haliss's action didn't surprise him, despite ordering her to return to the base. He knew she continued her contact with a whale she heard."

"Yes, I know. She let me hear it once. She communicated with it before she left me." He wondered how Haliss managed such a communication.

"Yes, sir. Haliss is staying, and the whale apparently agreed to host her."

"She really didn't want to go back into space."

Garcia continued. "Yes, sir. Maybe it will open up new understanding on the intelligence and communication skills of whales."

Lee felt happy for her. "You're right. It will."

"Anyway, Kreliss wanted you to know in case you had thought she committed suicide like the denbra did."

"Thanks."

"And the new kreon Leadership of Three wishes you all well, Captain."

"We'll need all the well-wishes we can get. Tell them thank you. Did we leave you enough supplies?"

"Yes, sir. There were some freeze-dried goodies already here, too." Garcia chuckled.

"Very good. Doc told me your group has sole access to the complex there for the next month."

"Yes, we do. It will make it easier for the delivery of their fuel."

"Take care of yourself. Zuved out."

The trip north proved uneventful. Lee reveled in his ability to imbibe his strong cup of cacao again.

They stopped first in Australia, where Doc talked to fellow scientists at the Antso nuclear research facility. Doc had perfected a plea based on the desire to build a fleet of nuclear-powered research subs. He pitched his idea, and they almost laughed him out of the facility until he showed the payment and confided the truth to a couple of his close Aussie friends. Kreon payment was a king's ransom of extraterrestrial high-grade gold ore. One world the kreons visited had gold sitting on top of the ground.

The Australians offered him several rods for the payment and a place on *Dragon* for one of their scientists when they returned to Antarctica. It was a good start.

The submarine sailed to New Zealand, where they bought a few more rods. They confided in a leading scientist, who by this time had talked to his Australian counterpart. Lee became part of the negotiation team, telling his story at each stop.

They made the longer journey to South Korea. There, they used the last of the alien gold and bought two more rods of nuclear fuel. The Korean lead scientist also accompanied the fuel to Antarctica as part of the deal. Dr. Hak Cho-Hee came aboard and immediately Lee felt the power of her presence, as well as her beauty. She spoke only a little, but he didn't doubt her abilities. "Dr. Hak, we have a cabin with another scientist, if you don't mind sharing. Or you are welcome to use my cabin."

She smiled. "I am perfectly happy sharing a cabin with a fellow scientist."

During dinner on the second evening, she asked to sit next to him. "Of course," he responded, scooting farther into the booth to accommodate her.

"This is a unique experience. How do you get used to not walking in the sunshine and fresh air every day?"

Lee couldn't help asking, "You live in Seoul, correct?"

"Yes, I do."

He said nothing else and after a moment she began giggling. "I think you were making a joke."

"Yes," he said with a grin. "Still, submariners are a special breed. We like it or we don't. I have always liked it, although I am the first to enjoy the great outdoors."

She nodded. "These alien people. What are they like?"

"You wouldn't be impressed to look at them. Did Dr. Wilson talk to you about them?"

"Yes, he told me what they looked like, a little of their history, as well as their dilemma. But he suggested I talk to you because you had more experience with them."

"So, he told you they are symbionts?"

She nodded.

"I served as a kreon host. The leaders wanted to see if humans could be hosts. By hosting Haliss, they learned what they already guessed—humans are not great hosts. Still, I learned that someone who could share my mind really had something to say." Lee told Dr. Hak more about his experiences with Haliss.

"And one of your people is going with them?"

"Yes. Dr. Garcia is very adamant about going with the kreon." Lee wondered at the viability of the scientist's decision.

Chapter Forty-four

More scientists boarded in New Zealand and Australia. The questions continued all the way to Antarctica.

Lee stood on the bridge with Mace, feeling the stinging cold and watching the frigid waters. When he thought he saw a whale breaching, he jerked up the binoculars to study it.

"There is no way you are going to tell which whale Haliss hooked up with," Mace pointed out. "Or even if she made it."

He let the binoculars rest against his chest. "I would like to think she did. And yes, I won't be able to tell." He stared out at the ocean a little more. "In some ways, I miss her."

Macon said nothing, and neither did Lee.

The waves started building, putting the boat into a rocking motion. Freezing pellets peppered the two men.

"Time to go below," Macon announced.

Lee nodded and climbed down.

Macon and the officer of the deck followed, making sure the hatches were secure. "Take her down to one hundred and fifty feet."

Once below, the rocking ended, and the rest of the journey remained smooth. The scientists stayed in conference the entire way to Antarctica, which suited Lee fine. He'd answered enough questions for a lifetime. "You'd think they had revived me out of the ice," he murmured to the cat as he scratched under her chin. Dihana lounged on his chest as he lay on his rack, trying to get some sleep. A soft knock interrupted his reverie. "Enter," he called out.

Doc came in and sat down on a folding chair. "You look comfortable."

"Trying."

"Another day to get there?"

"Probably closer to sixteen hours. It will be midnight, so we'll lay out at sea for a few hours until sunrise. I hear there's supposed to be some weather. We may have to stay out even longer. By the way, did you ever think we'd be helping alien hitchhikers when we started this project?"

"No, I didn't. While this is a fantastic opportunity, I hope it doesn't become the norm."

"Heaven forbid! Let's stick more with counting seals and whales."

***

The storm blew out to sea, and *Sea Dragon* sounded for a thinner layer of ice to break through. Lee watched as the men coordinated their readings with each other, and then with the diving officer. Hovering below and rising straight up to the designated spot was a tough maneuver, but he knew they could do it. He held his breath as the ship rose evenly, then punched through the ice.

Lee had already donned his arctic gear to help clear chunks of ice from the sail with the weapons officer. They climbed up and pushed the hatch open. It took them almost an hour to clear the ice, then other crewmen freed the forward hatch to pull out the components of the snowcat.

Bates led a crew of five men to load up the first shipment of fuel for the kreons up on a small sled pulled by the cat. Several of the scientists, including Dr. Hak, were going on this first run. More would go with subsequent runs of fuel.

The route started out in the same direction he and Meyers had taken to the volcano—the one leading him to a close encounter of the symbiont kind. Abysmally freezing weather still didn't thrill Lee, but at least he had the strength to do it this time. The end of the trip lay in a different direction, taking them to the caves where the kreon hid for a year. Their spacecraft sat just outside the main entrance. It appeared ready.

"Welcome to the kreon home away from home," Garcia greeted them at the entrance. He acted like a kid receiving his first cell phone.

"Hopefully, we have enough for them to fire up this jalopy and their mother ship out in the solar system," Lee quipped. The scientists who came with them couldn't take their eyes off the hosts. Soon, the alien and terrestrial scientists were in deep conversations with one another. The cat went back for the next load of fuel.

The kreons were eager to be away, especially since more humans knew of their presence. He understood their reticence to become involved with the various human governments. Lee couldn't figure how the different scientists had talked their respective governments out of sending military.

"Would you have believed a story like this if someone told you about aliens down here?" Doc asked.

He laughed. "No."

After several days of testing, the kreon urged their hosts to load up the ship as quickly as possible.

Garcia joined Lee and Doc as they grabbed snacks. His duffel bag clunked against the hard ground.

The two men gazed at him in surprise. Before either of them said a word, Garcia grabbed a couple of cookies and dropped in a chair. "They can't take me."

"It's probably just as well," Doc said to the forlorn oceanographer. "They'd always be worrying about whether they had the correct air, water and food for you, and those stasis chambers...."

"Yeah, I understand." Garcia sighed, nibbling on his cookie, then polished it off in one bite.

The alien ship launched the next morning, taking advantage of calm weather. It lifted gently like a Harrier, then shot straight into the sky, first appearing as a backwards meteor and then a disappearing star. The group camped out in the caves, feeling a comparative warmth from the semi-active volcano.

The scientists gathered what they could to study later, along with the pictures and notes they had taken during the past week. Lee, Bates, and Garcia curled up in their sleeping bags and fell asleep.

The walk back to *Sea Dragon* remained anticlimactic until they reached the broken ice near the boat. Garcia collapsed with a moan and a kreon slid out from under his sleeve. It moved with surprising speed under a broken piece of ice, disappearing into the ocean.

After a second of shock, Lee rushed to the scientist.

Garcia coughed, sucked in several breaths and then, with their help, sat up. "Mjir's host died just before take-off. He knew it was dying even before. It didn't want to go back into space either. Mjir wanted to do the same thing Haliss did. So, he contacted a cetacean and took a chance it would be in the vicinity. I hope it's close enough."

"Me, too," Lee added. "Then Haliss won't be lonely."

"Oh, she wouldn't be lonely with a humpback for a host," Garcia pointed out. With help, he got up and staggered to the boat, Doc helping him climb aboard.

Lee waited until the others were on board, including the scientists they had transported down to the continent, still staring out at the open waters. A whale breached in the distance. "Good luck," he murmured and climbed on board *Sea Dragon*.

Chapter Forty-five

Lee stood on the bridge, bumping elbows with the watch. It felt good to let the soft, warm breezes caress his face after their extended time in Antarctica. They were off the coast of Isabela, the largest island of the Galapagos Archipelago. Their assignment consisted in helping the Ecuadorian government study sea life in the deeper shelves.

Doc reveled in all the samples the scientists had gathered. Lee took this opportunity to dive in the shallower depths with the scientists. He needed to make another dive to test the limits of his gear. This time, they would go down after sunset. He heard of the amazing sea life coming up from the depths during the night. Garcia and several other scientists would accompany him, but Lee would be the chief photographer.

The sun hung above the horizon, so it wouldn't be long before the underwater show began. "Carry on, Stu."

"Aye, aye, sir," the young ensign replied.

Lee went below to check his equipment. Garcia and Farr carried down their gear, then pulled on their wet suits. Dr. Pamela Brighton checked her garish pink diving suit. Lee almost laughed but refrained. Brighton had probably paid a pretty penny for it. It had all the bells and whistles civilian money could buy.

Lee did a meticulous study of his steely gray Navy standard swim gear. He made sure the regulator worked; the tanks were full, and he had all the auxiliary gear he needed. The camera came next. Nice digital, state-of-the-art underwater camera.

"Sun will set within the hour," Garcia said. "Then the show will begin."

Farr appeared eager. He had already donned his wetsuit.

"Let's go out a little before dark," Lee suggested. "Then we'll get some nice video of the transition. We'll also be able to get a better picture of where we're diving and where any dangers might lurk."

"But we'll lose some of our exploration time, Captain," Garcia pointed out.

"We're only talking maybe fifteen minutes off the backside. We built plenty of time into the schedule for precautions."

"Sure, Skipper." Garcia grinned. "Then we need to get our butts in gear."

The group suited up and headed to the diving hatch. As only two divers at a time could fit inside, they went out in pairs. Brighton lived up to her name. She would be visible in the darkest night. The group swam below the *Dragon* and toward the upper shelf. Lee watched the various fauna as they swam by. Some passed by leisurely, while others scattered in apparent panic. A marine iguana undulated toward the shore, seemingly unphased by the four humans in their habitat. This area had been under protection for some time, so it would be natural for the animals to ignore visitors.

A seal shot past them and in the distance, Lee noticed sharks swimming in a group.

"We have you on the monitor," Wilson's voice broke into his reverie. "Sun is on the horizon."

"Okay, Doc," Lee answered. Although their technologically amazing diving helmets allowed for speaking, the divers tried to limit it. They didn't want to use up oxygen sooner than needed. "We're heading deeper."

They continued farther from the sub and beyond the shelf. Garcia led the way down the slope, his helmet light catching small creatures ducking away into crevices or hiding among corals. The sunlight above them continued to darken. Tiny glowing illuminations shone before them in the depths. Lee turned off his helmet light and watched as, like the stars in the night sky, they increased in density and brightness. Some of the organisms' lights glowed around their bodies, others pulsed up and down their spines, and still others had random lights, some on their fins or heads.

These ocean 'stars' rose toward them as the humans dove deeper and deeper. Lee felt surrounded by the living lights. The show entranced him, but he continued video-graphing as he had from the time they began their dive. He watched the organisms and hoped the video captured all the wonder of what they were seeing.

They reached a point on the shelf where it flattened out. Lee checked his depth gauge and found they were 135 feet deep. He motioned to the others, and they examined the dark shelf. Just to be on the safe side, they would give themselves a little more time on the ascent, but their suits could easily withstand this depth. He swam out more into the open to get extra footage of the incredible bioluminescent creatures. Large shapes loomed beyond his eyesight, but the camera caught them.

Brighton joined him. "The smaller animals come to the top and the larger ones come for a feast."

The deep-sea creatures rose to feed on the upper ocean creatures. A dance of the lucky getting the meal and the unlucky becoming the meal began. Lee gave her a thumbs up, even as he continued his photography duties. Brighton swam away, her colorful suit swallowed up in the darkness less than ten feet out.

He followed Brighton, the camera's light illuminating her as she worked. Lee paused when he saw Farr examining something of interest clinging to the shelf. Some sea fans and whatever lived in them. More video.

Garcia swam below about seven or eight feet, taking samples of various creatures swimming up from the depths. Lee saw several dark shapes, including a hammerhead. Then he spied another one.

"Garcia! Watch out!" Lee stopped filming and swam as fast as he could to the scientist. They each had shark repelling stun sticks, but with more than one shark, several might be necessary. He had almost reached Garcia when an even larger shape loomed close and scattered the sharks.

Lee couldn't see the end of the creature. Then he realized a baleen whale was checking them out. From the size, he figured it to be a humpback. He knew they migrated through this area but didn't realize there were any in the vicinity right now.

The whale stopped as though waiting for them to do something. It drifted closer. On a whim, Zuved reached out and touched its side. The creature didn't move. He swam along the whale's bulk, his fingers still touching its rough skin. Then he saw a familiar undulating shape crawling down the whale's side toward him. Handing the camera to Garcia, Lee pulled off his glove. The shape reached his fingertips and crawled up to rest on the back of his hand.

Haliss.

<Yes, Lee. As you can see, I made it.>

Yes, you did. I'm very glad. The other kreon seemed to think you would.

<Mjir made it, too. Another whale wanted to host him. We swim together.>

Are you learning from your new host?

<This is exhilarating, and I am learning so much about your ocean world. Selir is as intelligent as humans, but she can easily host me. I am glad I stayed behind.>

Selir is your whale host?

<Yes, she is. She has been telling me the tales of her ancestors and I have told her the history of mine. I am learning about your beautiful world, and she is learning about the stars. Is it not wonderful?>

Totally wonderful! I'm glad you contacted me. Did you follow Sea Dragon? *You know you could be our cetacean expert.*

<Selir is a skilled navigator and even if we go elsewhere for a season, it is easy to find something like your intriguing ship. And Selir and Srin don't mind as long as there is plenty to eat and no danger.>

Lee felt great happiness in her success. He could feel her happiness, too.

<By the way, Selir doesn't mind me telling you about her sea kin. She would like humans to know they are intelligent, so your kind will stop hunting her kinfolk.>

I know Doc will love learning more about Selir's people, as would I.

<We are going up to the surface. Srin and Selir are hungry, and this is the best time to find krill.>

Good hunting. Lee pulled his hand away as soon as Haliss had crawled back to the place where she rode the whale. He swam away a couple of yards while the humpback drifted toward the surface. There was only slight buffeting from the powerful creature's tail, but it amazed him how gently the whale departed. He studied his gauges and found they had maybe another hour of air left. His calculations told him they had half an hour of observation time before they had to return. Perhaps a little less to be on the safe side.

He motioned to an area they hadn't explored yet and took the camera back from Garcia.

"Was that Haliss and her whale?" Doc asked in his earpiece.

"Yes." Evidently Garcia filmed the interaction. Considering only he and Haliss could hear the communication, he figured to anyone else it would be boring, but not to Doc.

"You'll have to tell me what she said when you get back. By the way, according to the instruments, you'll need to return soon."

"I know. We're taking a few more videos and then we'll be back on board."

"Be careful, Lee."

He didn't respond. He checked the camera to make sure the memory card had enough space left on it and then continued filming. With the sophisticated lens, Lee got some incredible close-ups of the small bioluminescent creatures. He also filmed each of the scientists at their tasks. Then he called them to return to the boat.

As they swam up the sides of the Galapagos slope, Lee took more videos—things they missed on the way down. The amount and variety of life here amazed him.

The divers entered the same way they had left, through the escape lock. Two crewmen were nearby to help them out of their suits. Lee almost laughed at the attention Dr. Brighton had received. Perhaps that's the real reason she bought the bright pink and yellow diving suit. She used the inner hatch of the escape lock to change, while the rest of them dressed in the small diving storage room.

As soon as he changed, Lee took the camera to Doc's laboratory. He watched his boss download the material from the memory card and then store the card in a small safe in the wall. Lee felt weary from the long dive. Still, something piqued his curiosity. "Doc, you haven't given me any inkling of what's coming next. What is our next mission?"

"We don't have a paying mission until next month."

"I thought governments and oceanographic entities were climbing all over each other to get a piece of the *Dragon*."

"They are, but the government wants us to attend the investigation of the incident in Hawaii."

"Why the hell can't we give a deposition? Why sideline us?" Lee shook his head.

"I don't know, but as soon as we finish here, we're to head to Connecticut."

"How much longer will we be here?"

"Another week, maybe two."

"And the investigation won't start until we get there?"

Doc shook his head. "No. They start day after tomorrow. We'll be able to testify."

Lee nodded. "I'm going to get a little shuteye."

"As long as you four were out there, I can imagine. By the way, what's the word from Haliss?"

He passed along the conversation. "I suspect we'll have more contacts from her and Mjir."

"The whales have names? Even more evidence of their intelligence. Of course, it's going to be hard to explain where the information came from."

"For the moment, it will," Lee agreed.

Dihana strode into the room and meowed.

Doc chuckled. "I think your friend is trying to coax you to your rack."

"I am going to let her win this argument."

"Sweet dreams."

Chapter Forty-six

During the next several test dives, *Sea Dragon* dove to within two hundred feet of her five-thousand-foot limit without incident. Lee and Doc were ecstatic. The improvements to the sonar and cameras allowed them even better visuals than they had enjoyed during *Sea Dragon's* trials.

Studying the abyss on the monitors with the various strange creatures showing up from time to time almost had the scientists doing cartwheels. Most had not been into the depths except in cramped bathyspheres. Lee knew the scientific staff couldn't wait to review the materials and classify the creatures. He suspected some of them wondered if they were discovering new species. Their excitement rubbed off on him as well.

"Enjoy it while you can. We head to the east coast in two days," Doc announced to the executive officers. "We're reporting to the Galapagos conservationists tomorrow. Then we head to the east coast to testify in the federal trial against Roger Rollings."

Macon nodded. "As much as I hate sitting on anything like that, we need these poachers out of business."

The scientists who hired *Sea Dragon* to help with their surveys were extremely pleased. Videos, photos, and an enormous stack of data were enough for both the South American scientists and the *Dragon's* scientists to stay busy for some time.

After a long day, Lee headed to his cabin. He lay in the semidarkness of his small room, gazing at the ceiling, reveling in the freedom and satisfaction of the almost past year.

Lee woke up to the communicator squawking at him.

"Skipper?" One of the Petty Officers, Bill Namura, called. "Captain, sorry to wake you up, but we need you in the control room."

"Emergency?" He didn't hear any alarms.

"No, sir, but you're needed."

"Give me a few minutes." Lee slid out of his rack. His watch told him it was almost seven. He quickly washed up in the head, shaved, then threw on a clean uniform. He made it to the control room in less than ten minutes.

"What's up?" he asked Namura.

"Two whales cruising at the bow. They are staying away from the hull, but are almost acting like escorts. They have been with us since we left the proximity of the Galapagos. Dr. Farr said these were probably the same two whales you communicated with a few days ago."

Lee studied the bow monitors showing the two humpbacks keeping a safe distance in front of them. "He's right, except I communicated with the kreon the whales are hosting, not the whales directly."

"What's up, Lee?" Doc asked, appearing at his elbow.

"Haliss and Selir, Mjir and Srin. I think they are trying to tell us something."

"Why don't we go out and see what they want?"

"All stop," He ordered as they left the control room.

Patterson and Brown helped him and Doc with their suits. Lee went out first and found Selir waiting ten yards off from the boat. He swam in the clear water to Selir. Lee could see Haliss's form slither down and lay across his hand. *What's going on? Must be important for you two to get me out of bed.*

<I'm sorry, Lee, but we found something Mjir and I have never encountered before.>

Oh? What kind of something?

<Our companions were feeding near the surface, and we heard groaning below us. It resembled sounds Mjir and I have heard when a ship loses its hull integrity. The shrieking and crumpling of metal, but not the same. Selir did not recognize it either.>

Wilson swam right beside him, also touching Haliss. "Did you hear her, Doc?" Lee asked.

"I got the last part." *Where is this noise?*

<We can show you, Doctor Wilson. It's about five hundred feet below.>

Doc, please. How close did you get to this noise? Doc asked.

<We came close enough to see a glow near the sound.>

Any other phenomena?

<It interfered with Selir's and Srin's navigational senses. Disoriented them a bit. We did not approach too closely.>

Lee knew scientists believed humpbacks used a kind of magnetic navigation. Some scientists were discovering baleen whales had some of the same features as the toothed whales. Perhaps they used echolocation, too.

<They have both.>

How big was this thing? Doc asked.

<Selir could not tell, but the impression Mjir and I got was of something exceptionally large. As big as the circumference of *Sea Dragon*.>

Lee could tell from Doc's repeated questions his curiosity had taken over. *I think we should get some initial impressions, at least a hundred yards away.*

Yes, Doc agreed. *Let's head back to the boat and see if we can figure out just what this phenomenon is.*

Haliss crawled back up the whale's side and the two divers swam back to the *Dragon.*

Lee finished buttoning the top of his jumpsuit as he headed forward. "The two whales are still at our bow?"

"Yes, sir," Namura answered.

"Follow them. Ahead one quarter. If they increase speed, keep up with them."

"Aye, sir."

He watched the monitors and noticed Selir and Srin diving deeper. "Keep following."

Mace appeared at his elbow. "What's up, Lee?"

He told his XO briefly about the encounter outside the boat.

"What do you think it is?" the XO asked.

Lee shook his head. "No clue."

Wilson joined them. "It has to be electromagnetic if a humpback notices. There could also be a connection between the noises and the light."

"I guess we'll find out." Lee kept his eyes glued to the monitors. Just as Haliss had described, in the distance, he spied a yellow glow surrounding a circular flow of water. Like a whirlpool?

"Captain, I'm picking up noises—grinding, creaking, but louder," the sound man, Tam Nadill, reported.

Wilson put on a set of headphones and listened as well. "Like crunching an empty soda can, but on a larger scale."

"Ahead slow," he ordered.

"Something's messing up the sonar, sir," the sonarman, Levinsky, called.

"All stop!" Lee ordered.

The submarine shuddered, but still moved forward toward the strange, glowing mass. There was no sign of the whales. The yellow, glowing mass in front of them grew larger. "Reverse engines. Full!"

Lee really appreciated the monitors now. They were seeing the enormous mass, slowly swirling around a pitch black center *Like a black hole?* The *Dragon* shook.

"Can't sir. Something pulling us in," the navigator called out. He gripped the navigational yoke, leaning back, trying to get control.

"Keep trying, Corey. Full!"

"Can't, Captain! Engines are reverse full, but we're still being drawn in!"

Lee did a couple of mental calculations. "Twenty degrees port, all ahead … full." A calculated risk, but they might slip past the phenomenon. For a slight moment, it appeared they were going to succeed. Then, as though something had clamped onto them, they were pulled back toward the huge black eye.

"Sir, there is no navigation. Whatever this thing is, it's got us!"

"Battle stations!" *Dragon* shook harder and then rocked from one side to the other. The lights flickered and then went out. Red emergency lights came on immediately. Just before the boat tipped starboard almost fifty degrees, Lee remembered he had ordered full power. He called out 'all stop,' but it didn't matter. They passed through the black, gaping orb. Electrical systems popped and spit, but the sub otherwise passed through smoothly. Even the men held their breath. No screaming. No moaning or groaning.

Then Lee felt something squeeze him, pushing all the air out of his lungs. The blackness flickered again.

Chapter Forty-seven

Lee was still crouching over the navigational computers when his full awareness returned. The monitors blinked but stayed dark. The red lights overhead still bathed the control room in rosy softness, but there was nothing soft about the way his head felt. He stood up and gazed around. Several others held their heads. They groaned but remained conscious. The battle stations still blared.

"Turn them off and all stop," Lee ordered. The bow monitors remained dark, as were the ones showing on each side of the Dragon. "Tam, are you getting any readings on sonar?"

Lee felt the steady murmur of the propulsion unit as it slowed. Then it stopped. There were several other systems he could hear working in the background. That reassured him.

"Open ocean, sir," Levinsky relayed. "We are approximately a mile above the bottom and there are no landforms nearby."

"Thanks. Jerry, get the computers back online."

"Aye, sir."

"Sounding whales, sir," Nadil called out. "Sounds like a song."

"How many?"

"Two. I think it's our friends."

"So, they came with us."

Doc finally chimed in. "I hope to hell the vid cameras got some footage of that thing."

Lee grabbed the com link to speak to the entire boat. "All stations. We are not sure exactly what happened when we encountered this underwater phenomenon, but the *Dragon* seems to be intact. Systems are coming back online. All stations report your status."

Just as he finished, the monitors flickered back on. They were sharp and clear, showing a vibrant ocean with not only the two whales, but many other creatures, especially fish. They lay a hundred feet below the sunlit surface.

"Sir, I can get the computers up, but not the VMS (voyage management system)," Jerry said.

"What? No GPS?"

"No, sir. We have all internal systems, but nothing coming in and no communications."

"What the hell?" Mace muttered.

"We're going to have to surface, Lee," Wilson suggested.

"I agree. We can check the hull and get a better fix on our position." He gave out the command and noted everything worked perfectly as they rose to the surface. Lee went up the bridge first with his binoculars. The sun shone brightly enough to force him to squint against the water's glare. Two whales breached starboard, then swam close. Lee pulled out his cell phone and noticed he had no bars.

Scanning with the binoculars, Lee got his second surprise. He could see land, but much more distant than it should have been. They were only a couple of miles from the southwestern tip of Isabella in the Galapagos before their encounter.

Doc was next to him. "Something seems different. Can't place my finger on it."

He handed him the binoculars. "We're farther out from the archipelago."

"We were going full speed for a while, too."

"True."

The scientist pulled out his cell. "Can't pick up the conservation station. We could yesterday."

"Same here." Lee handed Doc his cell and then climbed down from the bridge, striding forward to the end of the bow.

One whale, Selir, he thought, drifted closer. She sang a few notes and gently bumped against the hull, soaking him.

"Thanks, Haliss—Selir." He decided they wanted to talk to him. Srin and Mjir stayed about twenty yards out. Lee pulled off his shoes and motioned Selir to back away. The whale accommodated. He climbed down a narrow ladder and swam closer. Haliss waited where he could reach her. The kreon climbed on top of his hand while Lee hung on to one of Selir's knobbles. Water slapped him in the face, but the whale lay in the water as quietly as she could.

<Selir says there is a different taste and feel to the ocean now.>

A different taste and feel? What does she mean? More pollutants?

<There are less. She also hears more ocean singers or inhabitants here than there were yesterday. From my position, my internal sensory indicators detect differences. Salinity, minerals, very minute.>

What are your conclusions? We cannot contact the outside world. All the Dragon's *systems are intact except for those using outside communication.*

<When our starship traveled from one system to another, we used interstellar gates or folds in space, allowing

us to get from one place to another. Perhaps this strange phenomenon, which we did not detect until yesterday, took us to a different world.>

What!!? We aren't on Earth?

Chapter Forty-eight

<This is most strange. Except for these minute differences, I would say we are right where we were a few minutes ago—on Earth. However, I cannot think of any other explanation. We are on a world very similar to the one we were on before going through the portal.>

Lee pondered her comments as he heard Doc calling to him. While he read avidly, he didn't have a great deal of spare time during missions. He remembered reading a novel about travelers crossing through some kind of portal from one universe to another. *A parallel universe?*

<Despite having traveled among the stars, I'm not familiar with the term.>

Could we have gone from the world we were living in to a similar one? One diverging and taking a different evolutionary path, whether a long time ago or recently?

<So, the underwater entity is some kind of gate or portal? Like our star gates?>

Could be, but we'd have to travel to a port to test our theory.

<And if it is?>

Let's cross that bridge when we get to it. Lee didn't want to consider being stuck in a vastly different world. *Let me talk with*

Doc and the other scientists and see what they think. Then we can plan what we're going to do.

Lee swam the few yards back to the *Dragon* and clambered on board. Patterson handed him his shoes, and he squished through the lockout trunk hatch, motioning for Doc and Mace to follow him. Once inside, Pat handed him a towel, and he wrapped it around himself. When they reached his cabin, he went in and pulled off his jumpsuit, grabbing a change of clothes from his dresser, while the others waited outside. Lee toweled himself off and dressed.

"What momentous thoughts passed between you and Haliss?" Doc asked when Lee invited them in.

Lee related everything he and Haliss discussed, including Haliss's idea. They had the same reaction he did. Then he told them his other ideas.

Mace stared at him. "Are you serious? A parallel universe?"

Lee shrugged. "This multi-verse thing is very popular right now."

Macon shook his head. "I know it is. I've seen the movie. But it's fiction. Like all these different Spider-people. It can't be real. Can it?"

Doc rubbed his chin. "Could we have done something like Haliss suggested? And we're in another part of the world? Or in another galaxy?"

Lee shook his head. "The readings say we're close to where we were before this fiasco. But we can test these baffling theories by heading for the Galapagos. And then someplace else to double check. Besides, Haliss didn't know of a star-type portal on a planet. Only in space."

Mace leaned against Lee's rack, his eyes showing confusion. "So, what the hell is going on? Maybe we're in the Twilight Zone?"

Doc sighed. "Might be the easiest explanation. I don't have any scientific theories for something like this."

Lee figured he needed to press forward even though he felt he grasped at straws. "Quiz time, gents. What happened to the Pevensie children when they found the wardrobe?"

"Huh?" Mace asked.

"You mean in the Chronicles of Narnia?" Doc clarified. "They passed from their English WWII reality to an alternate reality or universe. In the first book Lewis wrote, the wardrobe was the gateway." Then his eyes widened. "You aren't serious."

"Remember, I told you both whales detected some differences in the 'taste' of the ocean? Selir heard more 'singers' nearby. And I am assuming we still don't have any outside communications. Mace?"

The XO shook his head. "Not a peep. We are doing navigations using the CD's."

"Also, have someone take celestial readings as well."

Mace nodded. "As soon as we finish here. But if we made our way to another universe, what do we do now? And how will it affect the married crew?"

"We are three bachelors on an adventure," Doc began. "But six of my scientists have families stateside."

"About two dozen members of the crew have spouses or partners," Mace said.

"I'll make the announcement. Even though we don't have proof, I think we don't need to keep anyone in the dark. Who knows, maybe someone might have a less cockeyed theory."

Mace said, "I'll head to the control room and check out everything I can."

Doc sighed. "I'll talk to the scientists and feel them out, even though this is way out of anyone's league."

"Our resident physicist, Billy, might understand," Lee suggested.

"She might," Doc agreed. "We can meet later in the wardroom."

Lee finished dressing and made his way to the control room. It was a little less crowded than when they had gone through the hellish gate. He didn't look forward to making any announcements, but he had to say something. Lee would not keep the crew in the dark, even if he didn't know what they dealt with. Picking up the communicator, he began. "This is the captain speaking. I know you have all been wondering what happened and to be honest with you, I don't have a sure answer. However, the evidence points to," Lee took a deep breath, "some kind of transit from one multiverse to another— a parallel universe. It is only a theory at the present time. If this is the case, we will do everything, everything, in our power to return. And if anyone has a different idea of what we're dealing with, please come forward."

He shut off the call, then contacted Doc. "Have you met with the scientists yet?"

"Only long enough for a consensus to go back to the coordinates and see if the phenomenon is still there."

"Do you think that is the better option than heading to the Galapagos?"

"We're closer. Let's check for the gate and if it's not there, then we'll head back," Doc reasoned.

Lee gave the coordinates, and the boat prepared to dive. When they returned to the spot, the depths were calm, with nothing out of the ordinary. The two humpback whales crisscrossed nearby, surfacing occasionally to feed and replenish their air. "Expand the search outward for the next two hours, then report." He left for the wardroom, wondering if he should have kept his cushy executive officer's position.

Chapter Forty-nine

Doc and the other scientists were still talking when Lee entered the now-cramped room. He snagged a cup of cacao and threw in a little creamer.

"Someone tell me why we were investigating something like a dangerous phenomenon, anyway?" Grady Murphy, the geologist, growled. He was happily married thirty-something, with several kids, one born only a few months previously.

Doc glared at Murphy. "We were investigating a scientific phenomenon, Doctor. That's why we're here."

Murphy didn't pick up on Doc's stink eye. "Maybe the captain can explain why we were so close to it. And how I'm going to get back to my wife and kids."

Lee took a sip of his cacao. It gave him a moment to compose a calming answer. Now was not the time to discuss protocol or get into a blaming session. "We weren't close to it, or at least too close in relation to any other phenomenon we've studied. To be honest, we believed we were well back from it. The portal, or maelstrom, enlarged and advanced on us, then somehow pulled us into it. I know this sounds like a silly metaphor, but kind of like the phenomena envisioned on shows like *Star Trek*."

Murphy huffed.

"You said something about getting back home," Dr. Olafsen, one of the biologists, reminded him.

Lee nodded. She had become engaged to a handsome young doctor in Hawaii just before the Galapagos mission. "I plan on being optimistic, Maddie. We may not have a magical Aslan, wardrobe, or interstellar gate, but we are going to do everything in our power to get back. It brought us through. When we find it again, it should take us back home. The other thing to consider is we haven't proved we are somewhere different. Is this an alternate universe? There could be some other explanation."

"Like what?" Farr asked.

"I really don't know. We *all* need to keep working and contemplating what's happened," he continued.

Doc walked over next to Lee. "We thought surveying the area for that thing we came through would be a good idea."

"I agree, and we can leave a buoy in the vicinity, so if it's recurring, we have a sure-fire beacon."

Doc rubbed his chin. "What about one of the whales? What if one stayed nearby?"

"I don't know. I can ask Haliss. But if we are out of the area, would they be able to talk with each other? I never have asked how far they can communicate."

"Maybe a micro-communicator would help," Garcia suggested.

"Except most of them rely on satellite or tower transmission to cover the distances we might have to go," Lee replied.

Doc's eyes lit up. "We have a few of those micro-minnies. They only broadcast a signal. The transmitter is so powerful it can go halfway around the world."

"Again, I have to ask them. They may want to stay together."

"Your department, Lee," Doc said with a laugh. "I would suggest you put on a wetsuit this time."

"Oh, I will." He thought about their first destination. Now they had determined no full-time portal existed where they had come through. They wouldn't need to go as far as Guam or Juneau to prove they were some place other than home. Closer destinations, after they checked the Galapagos, might be the Panama Canal, maybe Pearl Harbor, or San Diego.

***

<And these micro-transmitters would keep us in touch?>

Srin fed a short distance away, but at a quick song from Selir, he swam closer. The whales communicated with one another. Lee wished he could understand their lyrical and soothing communication. Haliss climbed back on his hand.

<Srin said he would stay in this area where the device brought us through and alert us if the strange tunnel began operating again.>

Tell him thank you. The plan is to go to a place nearby where we might see if there are differences, proving our theory about an alternate universe. Or give us clues to returning home.

<Where might you go?>

We're going to the Galapagos first, then to the Panama Canal. Lee noted the darkening of the light. The sun had been lowering toward the western horizon when he left the boat. *I'll bring your transmitters tomorrow morning. Each of you will have one. The* Dragon *will pick up both signals.*

<We will see you in the morning, then.>

Lee swam back to the boat, entering through the diving hatch, where Patterson helped him out of his gear. "Thanks, Pat."

"Sir?"

"Yes?"

"What are we going to do if we can't go back?"

"Pat, I'm not even sure if we aren't already where we're supposed to be. A solar flare couldn't have knocked out communications." Lee saw the serious expression. "But if we are in some kind of parallel universe, I will not give up looking for a way back."

"Thank you, sir."

"Think positively. We came through. There has to be a way back."

"Yes, sir." Patterson didn't sound convinced.

Lee stopped by the wardroom where he saw Macon already there.

"Well, what's the verdict?" Mace asked.

Bates poked his head into the doorway. "You mind a bit of company, sirs?"

"Don't mind at all, Bates. Join the crowd. As to your question, Mace, the whales are okay with the plan, although they wanted us to all stay together. I told Haliss and Selir we'd bring out the micro transmitters tomorrow morning. I also told them where we are going to either prove or disprove our inane theories."

The others waited for him to continue. "I suggest the Panama Canal after we check out the Galapagos. Both are close enough to pick up transmissions from Mjir and Srin in case something happens here. Any of those places should tell us if we're in Kansas or not."

Bates nodded. "So, one of the whales and its kreon are going to stay in the vicinity and the other will accompany us."

"Unless anyone has a better plan," Lee said. "And don't be surprised if you're asked any 'what if' questions."

"Gotten a couple already, sir," Bates said.

"So have I. It's hard to answer someone whose loved ones are wondering where we are. Who would understand 'somewhere over the rainbow?'" Mace asked.

***

The next morning at first light, Doc supervised the insertion of the micro transmitters on the inside of one of each whale's pectoral fins. Both whales were as perfectly still as they could be, and Doc finished within a couple of minutes.

<There is nothing Selir or Srin need to do?> Haliss asked.

No. Is the transmitter interfering with either whale's navigation? Lee countered.

<No. They say they barely felt them going in.>

Good. We'll be underway by midmorning. I think the sooner we find out what's going on, the better.

<I agree with you, Lee.>

After changing into his ship's jumpsuit, he strode into the control room, hoping he sent out vibes of confidence. Then he gave the destination. The sailors and junior officers went into action. "Take us out, Lt. Irons."

"Aye, aye, sir," she responded.

Lee watched as the crew worked together, called out orders, and the boat headed toward the Galapagos. It only took a few hours. Lee and Chief Bates went topside as they passed by Isabella Island. They saw no trace of a research station, tourists, or even boats. No radio communications, no people at all. There were still no signals from any satellites. Occasionally, the communications officer picked up shortwave signals, but nothing anyone could make out.

"Plenty of animals, sir," Bates said facetiously.

"Notice how skittish some of them are?"

"Yes, sir. Like there's never been tourists here."

Lee scanned every direction. "I think we have our answer, but we'll head toward Panama."

"Aye, sir."

They both went below and Lee gave the orders to head northeast.

On the fourth day, near sunset, they were within thirty miles of the canal and running on the surface. They picked up more of the shortwave signals, but static kept them from figuring out not only what they were saying, but also where they were coming from. Since it sounded like Spanish, several of the crew who were fluent in the language began taking turns in the communications shack.

"Skipper, they're talking about some kind of airship crash," Ensign Montez finally said. "What I can figure out, a passenger airship out of New York City crashed in route to Raleigh. Many casualties."

"Airship, not airplane or jet?"

"Airship."

Lee just shook his head. "Well, at least New York City and Raleigh are still around. Keep listening. We'll get closer to the canal after the sun goes down, although we've seen no increase in activity." Lee continued feeling the sinking sensation of impending bad news he'd felt since they had checked out the Galapagos.

The sun set in a glorious golden glow behind them. In the distance, mountains rose out of shadows.

"I'm getting another shortwave station, but it's a language I can't quite figure out. Like a cross between Spanish and something else," Montez called out.

Lee listened to the static-filled voice speaking a language totally unfamiliar to him, and then music began. He tried to determine the type of music. It sounded closest to New Age. A flute gave it a Native American flavor.

"Eight miles out from the canal, Skipper," Mace said. "Except there aren't any signals. We should hear something by now. The Panama Canal is as busy as O'Hare Airport."

Chapter Fifty

"Continue slow, Mace. And by the way, you have the con. Consider me an annoying backseat driver." Lee felt Doc at his elbow.

Macon turned back to the instruments. "Aye, sir."

Dragon continued slowly. The monitors showed little or nothing, but a bow light displayed a school of dorado scattering. A shark chased after one, but the fish was too fast. The shark cruised down into the shadowy depths.

Their monitors showed them a vibrant reef just below. Ahead of them, the shelf rose.

"All stop," Mace called.

The submarine rocked gently. No one said anything, although there was muttering.

"I think it might be a good idea if a few of us went ashore to reconnoiter. Either our navigation is wacky, or we have found our definitive proof," Doc suggested.

"We're on course, sir," Bates said. "We're using a disc."

"Group of four. We'll take the light Zodiac," Lee announced. "I am one. Bates...."

"Me," Doc interjected.

"Doc and Montez. Let's go."

"Now?" Doc asked.

"We really don't know what we'll find out there. I think it would be better if we do reconnaissance where we can see but not be seen. I would really prefer to find out a little of what we're dealing with before we talk to any residents."

Doc headed forward. Montez followed, and Lee called for Bates to join them.

"What do you think we'll find, sir?" Bates asked as they inflated the Zodiac.

"Maybe a village, maybe jungle. Or both."

"So, you think we're in a different universe?"

"I don't know about the different universe, but we're somewhere different. Can't deny it, Chief."

"Where will we go next?"

Lee shrugged. "Not sure. There are a couple of possibilities. First, we have to decide how much interaction we make with folks around here."

"Yes, sir. We'll have to keep a low profile or there'll be lots of governments after *Dragon* and us."

"I agree, Chief. There is that possibility." Lee and the others strapped on their pistols.

Bates lowered the inflatable into the calm waters. The almost silent motor on the Zodiac took them within a quarter mile of the shore. There had been no sign of civilization until then, but now a few lights gleamed ahead and Bates shut off the motor. They took turns rowing the rest of the way in. At a point where the canal should have been gaping in front of them, bright from myriads of lights, only a sandy beach with trees greeted them.

Several creatures howled, creaked, whined, or croaked. Then they heard cows mooing. Bates jumped out of the boat just before it ground to the shore and pulled it in. Lee and Montez climbed out and helped. Doc waited until the boat stopped moving before he stepped out. Bates tied the boat up to the nearest tree and they each grabbed a flashlight.

They found a narrow path leading between the trees toward a house with a gleaming light in one window. Lee motioned them to stop before they walked into the clearing. He heard growling in front of the hut and didn't doubt it was a dog.

"Call out in Spanish," Lee whispered, "and tell them we're lost and need information."

"*Por favor, señor, estamos perdidos y necesitamos información!*" Montez called out. The dog bayed and prevented the ensign from repeating himself.

Lee stared in surprise when he heard the voice inside the small shack yell at the dog in English.

"Shut up!" A bearded man walked out on the porch and looked out toward the path, a gun in one hand and a lantern in the other. "¿Quién anda fuera?" he called out. The gun looked bulky and almost like some antique single-shot pistol.

The man didn't sound or look Hispanic. "We're lost. Can we come in and talk?"

The man paused a moment. "Yeah, come on in, but keep your hands in sight."

"Montez, stay close by. In case someone from one of those other huts comes to investigate."

"Aye, aye, sir."

Lee slowly stood up, as did Bates and Doc.

"Come on closer so I kin see ya' better."

Lee's toe jammed against an exposed root. "We're not familiar with your path. I'm getting my flashlight out."

"One of those gas jobbies?"

"Gas jobbies?" Doc muttered.

"No," Lee said tersely. He kept the light where the other two could see the rough spots on the path. Soon they stood ten feet in front the man. The dog, on a chain on the far side of the house, was pitching a fit.

"Shut up!" the old man roared. The dog quit bellowing but whined and pulled at his tether. The bearded man studied them. He straightened and then motioned them to follow him. "Come on in." He walked into the shack.

"Room in there for all of us?" Bates mumbled.

"If there isn't, Terrill, you can make friends with the dog. I think it would be a good idea for you to wait in the doorway, anyway. Keep watch."

"Aye, sir."

The two men stepped over the threshold. Lee's mouth dropped open. The inside of the shack was a submarine museum. Without getting permission, he stepped over to the wall. He examined the various parts and pieces he recognized as coming from a pre-LA class submarine. Lee tried to remember any lost submarines. SSN *Anglerfish*? First voyage in the Pacific. Somewhere east of Hawaii, according to the reports. Totally disappeared, no wreckage, no survivors. It had been a mystery that boggled the minds of every scientist and fortune hunter trying to find it.

Then he saw the plaque on one wall. Peering closer, the enormity of their predicament slammed the breath out of his body. In their own place, the place they had come from, *Sea Dragon* was now one of the 'disappeared under mysterious circumstances' ships.

"*Anglerfish*? Are you from the *Anglerfish*?"

The End of Book One

Coming soon!

Voyage of the Sea Dragon, Dance with the Devil.

Please consider writing a review for *Voyage of the Sea Dragon*. Reviews are very important for writers and readers.

Author Biography:

Susan Kite has been writing for thirty years. She wrote fan fiction for a decade. A visit to the Mission San Luis Rey in 2001 became the catalyst to write her first novel, *My House of Dreams*. *The Mendel Experiment* trilogy, *Realms of the Cat, Moon Crusher, Crossroads to the Stars,* and *First Realm* were all published by World Castle. The second *Moon Crusher* novel will be published soon. *Billy Bob Flybottom; a Very Tall Tale* was published by Doodle and Peck. Bold Venture Press published three Zorro novels: The Outward Journey, The Forbidden Country, and The Deadly Homecoming.

She worked in school libraries for 35 years. Now retired, Ms. Kite lives in Yukon, Oklahoma, with her husband, Dan; a chiweenie terrier, and two black cats, one of whom she named Zorro.

Website: www.bookscape.net